CUPID'S & CYTHE

EX LIBRIS

Venus De Mileage

2nd Edition

Tangleflower

CUPID'S SCYTHE

CUPID'S SCYTHE
(GRIM'S BOW)

BOOK I

**"Love and death are the two great hinges
on which all human sympathies turn."**

B. R. Hayden

FOUR WOMEN TALKING ABOUT LOVE

Four women were talking about Love, in different ways. The women drank wine, coffee, water. They argued for and against Love. Three of them were for it and gave impassioned speeches: as if Love was a cause to be championed, a worthy pauper in need of a "Friends of" clan whose benefactors would rattle cans and beg donations and signatures for petitions.

"There is no such thing as Love," Amy, the first woman, said. She claimed she'd never been in it. She'd never been in the sea but she knew it existed, she'd seen it and seen others in the summers of their lives laughing and diving down into it, holiday makers full of whelks, waiting for the splash, plunging in, despite the perils of filth and fearsome beasts. But with Love it was different. She'd never seen anyone in it. She'd never learned to swim and feared drowning.

"I believe in Love at first sight," said the second woman, Bryony, her wantful eye on the waiter, her hopeful heart swelling her breast. She looked about the restaurant for Cupid, peering through her spectacles with intent as if squinting her eyes and really focusing might somehow conjure him. Cupid was not there. It's not like in the movies, she thought, as imagined arrows missed her, again.

The third woman, Christina, said, "Love should be forever." She was steeped in three-weeks' worth of ardour from a man who would be gone away the next day. Forever. Love came and stayed awhile, but would not outstay its welcome. The three-week man had expensive tickets to Somewhere in the pocket of his expensive jacket. He would leave a note on her bed, and a bunch of loud afterthought flowers in unthoughtful colours. £4.99.

No one said Love was a sickness. No one said it was a disease or a madness. Not even Daryl, the fourth woman, and she knew well enough that it was an incurable condition. She knew it could send you crazy. Love, she claimed, is the thing that makes you afraid of death, your lover's and your own. She sipped her wine. She said, "You're unlikely to die together. One of you must be left behind. It's madness." There are natural, if unfair, orders of things.

1
THE BONES OF LOVE ARE BEAUTIFUL

Love *feels* like forever. It feels like nothing else. Fall into it, or think of it as ascension, nothing will ever feel quite the way It does. It makes the world look different.

Daryl left the restaurant alone, leaving her three friends analytically stripping the flesh from the bones of Love.

They supped wine and water and coffee.

They ate chocolate ice-cream, though Christina said she shouldn't really.

The bones of Love, bared, are beautiful. They are True.

2
THE BONES OF LOVE ARE
NOT BLEACH-WHITE

The bare bones of Love are not bleach-white. They are not blanched, not Natural History exhibition bones. The bones of Love are stained. Amy, the first woman, the one who didn't believe in Love, didn't like walking along the promenade in harsh weather. The salt from the sea left white indelible tides on her black suede boots.

3
FLESH HANGS FROM THE BONES OF LOVE

Flesh hangs from the bones of Love.

Even when Love has been gnawed away at, there are still those stringy bloody slivers attached to its carcass.

Unhard, life-ful things full of hope.

Bryony, the second woman, the one who believed in Love at first sight, smiled (again) at the waiter and longed for a yawning purple hole to appear in her heart.

"Cupid's arrows are blunt," she said.

4
LOVE WARPS TIME

Love makes time warp itself. It makes a fool of the respected clock and the accepted calendar. It melts days away. It stretches day's reluctant limbs. It is bigger than measurement, more powerful than muscle; it is cleverer than we are. Daryl knew this. She had sucked the marrow from the bones of Love and lost her watch. She had fallen and ascended up and into Love.

5
THOUSANDS OF WORDS

Other people's love letters are over-egged puddings, lilies gilded, incomprehensible to other people. Daryl had written thousands of love letters, to one person. She hoped that neither she nor her lover would become stupidly famous. She baulked at the thought of her thousands of letters being published. She baulked at the thought of her lover's words to her being read by strangers. She believed that together they had written the Book of Love... at hotmail.co.uk.

Truth is it's only possible to write of love in the blood of gods with the quills of angels. Even then, words don't always live up to expectation.

6
ALL'S FAIR IN LOVE AND WAR

Amy doesn't believe in Love. Silly unreal Love. And the other women all have very different and fixed ideas of what it is, of how it should be.

So, let's have a laugh. Dress Love up as the Grim Reaper. Why not? Give Love a scythe.

See Cupid, with his well-meant arrows, shrieking his little angel cries in fear? Let these two, Death and Love, swap weaponry. Masqueraders masquerading as one another.

On your marks, get set...

A mischievous god pulls the trigger on the starting gun. And the games begin: This is war, this is Love, so all's fair...

Reaper licks the cherub's bow, tongues the arrow sharp. Cupid cuts his finger on Death's oil-black unfamiliar blade.

On the way home from the restaurant Amy remembers a childhood crush suddenly. She salves the scorch of memory with thoughts of library books that need returning and windows that must be cleaned. She doesn't know quite what she believes now. But she knows things hurt.

Push it all away.

Hope it stays away.

7
LOVE OR DEATH – DEATH OR LOVE

Love worms into you. It's the thing that makes you hum tunes you loathe and know the words of songs you'd once condemned as slush.

Reaper holds the angel's pretty bow and pretty arrow with surprising elegance.

Cupid uses plasters and *Savlon* to heal the wounds caused by his ineptitude with the Reaper's tool. He's out to get you.

The Reaper is the nice guy now.

Love or Death?

Death or Love?

8
LOTS OF LOVE

When Christina, (she believed Love should be forever) found the flowers on her unmade bed she cried. Their garishness clashed with her pale and stylish idea of herself. And they were already wilting. She put them in water, gave them an aspirin to thin the blood of their hearts, to keep their hearts beating for extra time. Ever hopeful. She didn't see the Reaper at the window. She was too busy reading a note. In the morning the flowers had sprung their gaudy heads up, grateful for her attentions, appreciative of her sweet attempt to keep them going, keep them alive. They stared at her and she felt guilty for disapproving of their common colours and their in-your-face ways.

She threw the accompanying note in the bin. It had said, amongst other things, *lots of love*. Lots of Love clearly wasn't very much Love at all. It clearly wasn't Love.

It rained. On and on. Christina couldn't sleep. She filled the flooding night with a rerun film that ran and ran relentlessly on Sky. Blue-eyed actor and red-lipped actress fused to one another like molluscs to a rock. Screen kisses never miss. That sort of Love *is* forever. Just rewind and play again. And again. Frames frozen and thawed.

The Reaper ha-haa'd his breath onto her window pane and fingered a jagged heart-shape into the mist he'd made. His first tentative scratchings.

Cupid smiled a gargoyle smile. He was watching.

9
A FLOODED NIGHT FILLED

Bryony sighed, stretched, checked to see if morning was at the window yet. Tomorrow, she thought, I'll change my image, have my hair re-styled, re-coloured. I might even get designer specs.

Cupid's bare feet made imprints on her wet lawn. He fumbled, with bandaged thumbs and bloodied fingers, with Reaper's heavy chopper, dragged it behind him so it scarred the grass and left a Tullish trench; a furrow neat and deep enough to sow seeds in. Seeds of Love, or Death's spawn? Little boy with a big boy's toy.

10
REAPER AND CUPID GET A
FEEL FOR THEIR NEW ROLES

Reaper and Cupid start get a feel for their new roles.

Cupid's modest tools, his artful arrow and his bow, fit tidily in Death's designer pocket. The Reaper, grim though once he was, has un-cowled his wicked head, slipped his shroud. Reaper has smartened up. He's looking suave now in black shades and white suit. He's cutting it. Hell, who'd have thought it, he's even wearing a cravat; red silk - as red as the red bloods he'd once shed.

Cupid, empowered *enfant terrible*, can brave off bullies with his blade. It makes him feel bigger and stronger than he is because it's bigger and stronger than he is. He's an apprentice in the Death business now. But the Reaper's scythe was built for the seven-foot tall Reaper. It was honed for *his* expansive hand; a hand with the span of a predatory bird's wing, an elegant long-fingered hand that can block the light from a moon, or dim a sun. A hand that can wring equally effectively a strong or a fragile neck.

Cupid with a scythe. A baby with a broadsword. At night the cherub practices wielding his new weapon. Beneath stars. On empty beaches where the red of his first mistakes will wash away through stones and sand, through weeds, past unknowing fishes. He likes the power, he laughs and laughs and laughs and laughs. But the blade has every act of annihilation tooled into its metal. It catches one of Cupid's wings, slices the imp's ability to fly straight, slices his ability to think right, to think as he once did.

He limps now.

Licks wounds and lips.

Cupid weeps.

He wants to kill.

11
THE END OF A LONG SHORT DAY

Daryl spent the day with her lover.

It was the longest day. It was the shortest day.

They made Love in places they shouldn't, in ways she hadn't known were possible. It was as if this Love of hers had introduced her to her own body. Her own self. She saw a different Her in the mirror when they'd been together. Felt a different Her.

They went to a churchyard because they liked the architecture of churches, the mossed artistry of graves and tombs. They went to a churchyard but they didn't believe in

11

God. She couldn't believe in anything but the 'Us-ness' of them, in anything but Love, their own love. She thought its power usurped all gods, but not all is fair in love.

The ground was scattered with jigsaw puzzle pieces. New blue shapes, arms and legs outstretched, strewn on old stones and new-grown, just-mown, grass. Puzzle pieces by the puzzling old graves of the long dead.

Had there been a wedding? Was this contemporary confetti? They found two pieces that fitted together. One for each of them.

They each took a puzzle piece home at the end of the long short day.

12
SCISSOR AND SCYTHE

There's not a word that sounds like scissors biting through hair. This is an onomatopoeic deficiency.

Bryony had her long hair cut short, watched psychometric years slink away to the floor. *Shooonk. Shoonk.*

Was she going anywhere nice for her holidays?

No.

She had her browns made red. She could be someone else now.

Cupid liked this woman with her head on fire. He could spot her in a crowd easy as anything.

There's not a word that sounds like scissors biting through hair.

There's not a word that sounds like a scythe blade slicing through a throat.

Shh

Shooznnnnk.

XIII
THE SCENT OF A SMALL AND QUIET DEATH

The flowers had faded to brown now.

It had been two weeks. Their petals had turned to parchment after a week but Christina couldn't bear to throw them away. She knew they couldn't stay alive forever. Not like the kind of Love she dreamed of finding. But if they'd just lasted a little longer... something to hang onto. Fake flowers were eternal. Real things died. The flowers had drunk all the water, had begun to stink.

Reaper recalls the cloying stench of death. Even the small and quiet death of cut flowers leaves a scent. He aims the arrow. Runs his eye down its length, wonders what it would be like to spear the dying flowers, crack the vase they're dying in... or pierce the woman's heart. He's tempted, but the time isn't right. He'll wait. There's so much he doesn't understand about Love.

Reaper's got a hard on.

14
STRANGUAGE

My Darling, my Love, wrote Daryl when she got home after the long short day. *It was wonderful, magical, being with you. Am still laughing about the disapproving squirrel, the missing shoe and the terribly unhelpful ticket man at the station. Remind me never to eat noodles on a Wednesday again. There's a mark where you bit me. I hope it stays there until we see each other next time. It hurts and reminds me of you. Oh, the little book is beautiful. Thank you. I Love you I Love you I Love you. Have you put your puzzle piece somewhere safe? Mine is under my pillow with the photograph of you with the stone penguin – remember that day? There's that thing on TV tomorrow, late. Don't forget. I'll try to record it but you know I usually end up pressing the wrong buttons so don't rely on me, baby, will you? Have to scoot, desperately need a pee; have done since I got in. I adore you, I am entirely devotedly awestruckedly yours. Yes, yes, I know awestruckedly isn't a word. There aren't the words...*

This is the language of Love. It's *stranguage* – you can't always say what you want to. Words won't let you. They are inadequate. Write them with the quills of angels in the blood of gods and they'll still fail you.

The language of love is strangled. And this is not your language anyway. It's hers. *Theirs*. It is their code. It makes no sense to anyone else. Sometimes even they cannot decipher one another. It isn't as full-blown as you might expect. It has the everyday peppered through it and the pain of bites. It's as if Love is some kind of "in joke".

Ha ha ha hurt.

Reaper sees Daryl at her computer, she smiles as she types. Reaper sees Daryl's lover miles and miles away, smiling, reading. Reaper thinks that Cupid, his juvenile predecessor, and *now* his successor in matters of death, did a good job with these two. He knows so little. Reaper is in the Love business now. His newly grown just trimmed moustache looks debonair. He stops to smell roses. He finds himself humming jolly tunes. He smiles and says good-morning, good-day and good-evening to the world. If he had a hat he'd doff it at you. He is the best mannered ex-murderer you could ever meet. A gentleman.

15
THE DOG

Reaper watches Amy. Amy takes her unread books back to the library. She pays a late fine. It's unlike her to be anything but punctual. She walks home the long way, down streets she doesn't usually go down. Past greengrocers and halal shops. There's a dog in the window of a pet shop she's never walked past before. She wonders how much it is. She wonders about getting a dog. Perhaps even that one. A living thing to live life with. She goes inside, ignores the foul-mouthed parrot, smells the smells of meal and millet. There are lovebirds in a cage. Trapped. An enforced union, dictated devotion, a menagerie marriage.

Cupid has followed. He's in the shop.

Human eye can't see him.

"Who's a naughty boy then?" calls the parrot.

"I am," says Cupid, stabbing the scythe's handle into a sack of chicken mix.

Human ear can't hear him.

The parrot falls silent. Eye on Cupid. The blushing birds stop their cooing and give out vulture cries; this is their new song, a battle cry. Birds' eyes on the Reaper, he's there too.

16
TWISTED

Death's in a happy frame of mind. He's the new philanthropist. And Love's cherubic ambassador has a killer's instinct now. Newly-appointed infantile executioner.

Things are all turning about.

Things are changing.

17
VENUS

Galileo groans and moans in his ancient grave: an old man in his bed, waking too soon. The planet Venus has plans to cast a shadow on the sun.

18
REAPER AND CUPID WATCH

The dog wants to go for a walk. He tells Amy this. He barks at her. He runs to the door. Whines. He has needle teeth. He has already chewed the leg of her coffee table. He has urinated on her carpet and his eyes look sorry.

Amy doesn't know why she bought the dog. It was so unlike her. But lately she has become... altered. She doesn't know what it is. It's like she's letting go. Or being let go of.

Reaper knows. Cupid knows. Things are changing.

The dog keeps barking at nothing. The dog keeps barking at corners.

Reaper and Cupid watch.

19
DEATH - QUIET - LONELY

Christina phones Amy. Had she seen that thing on TV the other night? Amy hadn't. The new dog had dragged her out of the house and made her walk along the seafront. Anyway, she wasn't into astronomy. "Neither am I," said Christina. It had just been an excuse to call. Loneliness is deathly quiet sometimes. Amy said she had to go; the new dog was chewing her best shoes.

Christina throws the dead flowers away. She'll buy herself some more tomorrow, to cheer herself up.

Reaper likes lilies best. Well, he used to - in wreaths.

20
BE SEEN, BE SEEABLE, GET SIGHTED

Bryony kept catching sight of herself: in mirrors, in shop windows. She was everywhere. She wondered, Is that me? Am *I* that woman with blood-red hair and designer glasses? She bought herself a jade green dress, then shoes to match. Expensive shoes. A treat. Now that her colours were brighter she felt more noticeable. She *was* more noticeable... and someone was watching.

Reaper was watching. And someone else...

Love at first sight? You had to be someone someone would want to look at for that to happen. Be seen, be seeable, get sighted.

Bryony'd seen a TV programme the other night. She didn't understand anything about the universe, but there was something promising and romantic in it, she thought.

Venus.

21
SHADOW

The planet Venus has plans to cast a shadow on the sun.

22
FLEDGLING THUNDER

Cupid never writes home these days. He is too immersed in the new him. Sweet narcissism. He's getting better with the scythe; it almost seems to fit him now.

The night before he'd hacked a tree down; an oak that had stood in a forest for one hundred years. He couldn't fell it with a single blow; it took one for every year of the tree's life. Assassination of a century's memories. Cupid smiled at the destruction he had made. His wounded wing was healing, growing strong again, and his form was changing, he was becoming leaner. Soft baby to sinewy boy. Even when he laughed his voice sounded different, there was fledgling thunder in it now.

Cupid fled the forest, flew across the moon. A witch shadow. His wings were black now, charred. He had work to do. He had his eye on the woman with the bright hair. Bryony. So did the Reaper.

And in the hundred rings of the slices of tree, an image, vaguely, formed of sap and stain and years of growth and history, a picture: a skullhead with heart around it. Death shrouded in Love, or Love with Death at its centre.

And soon...

23
REAPER RIDES THE NIGHT

Reaper acquires a fedora. A doffingly good piece of millinery. He cuts a dash, wears a crimson rose in his buttonhole. He picks the remnants of a decadent meal from his grin, hooks bits of caviar from his gaps with Love's dainty tool. Reaper strolls through the evening. He is only seen if he wants to be seen. Reaper rides the night bareback. Then...

Amy stirs, nearly wakes, to unknown feeling. Something there *between*, down below. Pushing, rubbing. The Reaper has thrust his foot in her hollows, scuffed away the frigid moss. He buffs his shoe on her vulva, shines it to a slick high gloss with her juices. The dog growls. Amy moans. Awakening.

24
INVITATION

Daryl plans a party for the day of the eclipse. It's weeks away still but she wants to spend it with her lover, and with friends, wants to be with those she loves on the day Venus inks her mark on the sun. So sentimental. She invites Amy and Christina. We'll eat outside, she says. She can't get Bryony on the phone. She'll try again tomorrow.

26
STARS OF STARS

There's talk on the TV and on the radio. There are reports in the papers. Only X amount of days to go now. Astronomers are in their element. They do like a celestial event. Major planetary things bring their science into everyone's living rooms. Making stars of stars and celebrities of planets. Venus will get her fifteen minutes of fame.

27
STRINGS ATTACHED

Reaper watches Bryony, observes her with a voyeur's smile when she wakes, when she sleeps, when she wakes again. "Ha," he says, you believe in Love at first sight. It's what you want. It's what you'll get. I can grant your wish." Bryony doesn't hear him. When she shops he follows, watches her. When she works, scratches her head, sharpens her pencils, cleans her palette, has a bath, he watches her. He imagines he has attached strings to her joints, imagines pulling them. Her legs, this way and that, her arms up and down, windmilling round. He imagines attaching strings to her mind, likes the idea of possessing her, of manipulating her emotions. Bryony feels odd, less in control, as if something unseen, unheard, approaches. Cupid, still light-footed, lurks.

28
TIME

Daryl's lover wrote: *Superb idea about Venus day, darling. I just got my schedule and I'm not working at all that week so will be home. I'm almost jealous that we have to have the Macbeth Three over. I'm protective of our time together. I adore you.*

29
DREAMS FEEL REAL

Amy had started to break rules, her own rules. Dogs weren't supposed to sleep on beds. Sod it. It was comforting, and she liked the dog. His breathing coaxed her own into a calmer rhythm. And she was a woman alone. The dog would guard her. Make her feel safe. She'd had some weird dreams lately. They were not like dreams at all. They affected her, physically.

30
THE MAN

The man:

The man's mother had been a redhead. Not a natural one, though he hadn't known that as a child. He'd never seen the mismatch of her glorious scarlet crown and pale brown blush of her mound.

He didn't think he'd ever seen this red-haired woman before. He didn't know she'd changed her hair colour. He thought she'd fallen, like an angel, from the clouds. Just for him. Thrown aflame and newly bloomed from a hothouse heaven, a just-cut crimson flower. Slave of Her flung to the Lion of Him. The man, we'll call him the Stalker because that's what he's about to become, smiles.

31
VENUS PLANS

Earth's volcanic sister plans to show her shadow on the sun. Just to let Earth know she's there.

32
ASPARAGUS AND CHOCOLATE

Daryl makes a list of aphrodisiac foods. She's planning a banquet for the Venus day party. She still can't get Bryony on the phone.

Amy has called back (she'd love to come). She asked if it was all right to bring the dog.

"It'll just be the two of us," she says.

She's never been able to say that before. It's always just been just the one of her. Amy.

33
A WARPED VERSION OF LOVE

The Reaper grins. He's given Bryony a mystery admirer: someone who has fallen heel-over-crazy-fucked-up-head into his own warped landscape version of Love with *her*, at first sight. It's what she wanted. She'll believe Love can happen this way.

But is this, is this *Love*, little more than a pretty path to Death? The scenic route.

Come along for the ride, enjoy the journey. Unfasten your seatbelts.

Cupid wants a trial run, but does not want yet to use his power on Bryony. He wants to taste other deaths before hers. Best til last.

He's a demi-god gone semi-mad.

34
?

Daryl and her lover don't live together. Her friends don't understand. People never understand the ways other people love and live.

35
LE PETIT MORT

Amy's dog makes her laugh. He has warm human eyes. And now a human name. He has toys, a collar with a tag and a special paw-print blanket all his own which he has chewed to a comforting tatter.

Amy really likes this dog. I like you, she says.

Reaper is proud.

Amy is starting to *feel*.

Is this what Love is about, the Reaper wonders.

Amy had her first orgasm last night.

"Yes, yes... *yes*," she cried quietly.

"Yes," said the Reaper, growling, fondling himself through the white linen of his suit trousers.

Is *this* what Love is about?

Love. Death.

Death. Love.

Sex.

The little death.

36
ARMY

Cupid sees the lads with hairless heads on the corner. He laughs to himself at their menace mask faces. One has a tear tattooed on his cheek. It seems to weep from his soulless eye. He makes a grotesque pierrot. Cupid laughs at the overshot jawlines and the drugged dead-fish eyes. An army armed with malice, cracking jokes and knuckles, smoking crack. They wanna kick someone's head in tonight. Just because. It's what they do.

Cupid surveys his new world from a roof top. He doesn't like the army's uniform, despises this ineloquent madness, this moronic bastardry.

37
DISCOVERY

Stalker finds out where Bryony lives. At night he sees red hair on white pillow.

38
FROM WANT TO NEED

Christina bought silk flowers for herself. They'd last longer than real ones, longer than forever. She bought books in a second-hand shop and wondered who had read them before her. She saw Amy walking her dog. "I really like this dog," said Amy to Christina. "*Really*. I do."

Is Liking a prelude to Loving, part of the progression? Hunger to Starvation. Want to Need. From Have Not to Have.

To Have and to Hold.

39
CUPID VISITS DEATH'S MANSION

Cupid flies by night up up high and up higher still across the universe. A bird in morbid migration. His shadow scars the planets. He looks down at the fragile speckled egg of Earth. He orbits moonless Venus and the moon itself and wishes wicked wishes on uncountable seas of stars. Sees the closed gates of Heaven and dives...

...down until Heaven is all but a memory. A memory forgotten. Down he flies, down to the Below. Past what's Without, into what's Within. Past Hell's open ravenous mouth. Hell's fire singes Cupid's wings; its heat scorches his eyes. Cupid visits Death's mansion.

He stands at the door. He doesn't knock. He has the keys. A killerman's house is his castle.

40
THE JEALOUS REAPER

The Reaper is only seen if he wants to be seen. And he wants to be seen. He's sick of seeing Cupid depicted everywhere; in books about Love, on greetings cards, in paintings. He's *so* popular. Those pretty girlish boys always are.

Reaper says to the unlistening world: I am the Death, your Reaper. I am a jealous Reaper. He doesn't know how to be the new him. Reaper cries dry tears. He is misunderstood.

41
NO VELVET CURTAIN

Death's house is cold and still as an unrobbed tomb. A soundless crypt.

The boy Cupid is a morphed moth, drawn to its *un*flame. Cupid's bare feet tread the bone dust on the floors of

Death's house. Kicking up the stardust of saints and sinners all long since decomposed, demised, gone to a whisper. Cupid breathes death into his nostrils like a drug. The fine and final powder of decayed things. Millions of years. Millions of dead things left to die more, die again. Death's midnight is no velvet curtain.

42
RHYTHMS

Stalker finds out:

- what times Bryony goes out
- when she comes back

He fixes the routines of her life to his own, the rhythms of her days pulse in his brain.

43
UGLINESS

The malice army boys are drinking courage out of cans now. Their dead-fish eyes are redder and deader than ever but these beasts are too unstreamlined to be sharks. They lack the elegance, lack the shark's focus. They have none of the shark's cool sneering beauty or awesome power.

One of them, the one with the tear tattoo, fucks a girl in an alleyway, attempts the unimaginative in-out-in-out action with his half-hard, half-hearted prick. It's a thing as pale as the white flab on an uncooked Sunday joint. Five minutes and he's spilled. If the others knew, he'd be a laughing stock. His prick, drugged spent worm, is tired and lacklustre. He fancies a kebab now to get his energies back up. Fat ineffectual gristle fuels fat ineffectual gristle. He might even have another go on the girl, Donna, the little slag.

"That kebab, it'd have to be a *doner*, eh!"

No one laughs.

"Get it, doner - Donna?" he says, pleased with his pathetic comedic turn.

44
VIRGIN BLOOD

Stalker knows what time Bryony goes to bed. Red head on white pillow. Like virgin bride's blood on a wedding bed sheet.

45
THE LONGING

Daryl misses her lover, but work is work, and life is life, commitment is commitment. There are situations, and these things sometimes keep those who wish to be together apart. Her lover misses her too. She thinks.

46
DEATH IN AMORE

Reaper's pissed off. He's been watching Christina flicking through the books she'd bought. A story of Love, but not a love story, with that damned little Cupid on the cover, all peachy-cheeked and impish. Don't you just adore him? No. And another book – *The Real Face of the Tarot*. And there *he* was. The Reaper. A whole chapter on Death. Words, images. The invented history, the misinterpreted history of him. An unauthorised biography. The disadvantages of celebrity. People think they know you. But they don't.

The jealous Reaper mocked.

Saw himself.

Death as a skeleton.

Death in his amorphous almost priestly robes.

Feared. Even… Death on a white charger. Poetic licence. A whimsical idea. The Reaper likes it.

Death in armour.

Time for change.

Death in Amore.

Christina believes Love should be forever.

Reaper knows that only one thing is forever. And he *was*, is still despite the garb and the new tools, the obdurate king of that bleak eternity.

47
STALKER KNOWS BRYONY'S NAME

Stalker knows who Bryony banks with. And he knows her name now. It is an ever-present whisper in his head. It sits on his tongue like a plump frog on a lily pad. One day he will speak her name *to* her, in her ear, into her fireblood hair. He says it out loud when he masturbates, says it louder, a desperate battle cry (for this *is* war) when he ejaculates, when he manages to. He can't always cum, but when he does, afterwards he is left feeling guilty, hollow, sullied. Ashamed.

48
SILENT MUSIC

The timber bones of an organ stand in Death's house. Like a monument. Cupid touches the aged keys, the remaining ivory teeth, the ebony teeth, with scabbed fingers that have never learnt to play. Silence. All the songs have been sighed out of this instrument. Cupid would have liked to hear death put to music.

A symphony for the sleeping.

A refrain for the resting.

A ballad for the bucket kickers.

A canticle for the croaked.

A Number 1 hit for the six foot under brigade.

49
THROWN AWAY

Stalker knows:

- what Bryony eats
- what paper she reads - she never completes the crossword, but she always starts it with good intentions.

Stalker finds the evidence of her days sweating in black sacks in a bin outside her house. He paws through the scraps of her single-girl-diet of lazy things in lazy boilable zappable bags. He envies the men in their high-vis jackets whose job it is to take her rank detritus away. He hates the fact that they think it rank, that to them it is merely detritus. They have the privilege of her delicious waste but they appreciate neither the honour nor the discarded gifts. This angers him. Anger makes his cock twitch and kick.

50
CUPID MOUSE

Cupid feels at home here in Death's vast echoing halls.

New boy strutting old domain, quiet as a mouse.

The cat's away…

51
LOST

Amy is calling her dog, calling his human name. But he hasn't come back into the house from the garden, and she can't see him or hear him. Perhaps he's slipped through a hole in the fence, slipped out into the world. She calls his name again. She will call and call and call. She stands at the back door and shakes the tin with his biscuits in. She longs for him to come back. She really likes this dog – she likes this dog a lot. The traffic growls and roars. Amy knows the roads are long and dangerous, she's walked them.

52
FAMILIARISATION

Stalker knows who Bryony's best friends are.

All three of them:

1: Amy 2: Christina 3: Daryl

53
WARRIORS

On the corner where the petty war is planned, the army recruits more ugly warriors.

More of the same. More like them. One has HATE on his left hand and LOVE on his right. Troop of grotesque doppelgangers. Apart from the tattoos you can't tell one from another. They won't be missed, so Cupid thinks. There are scabs on the knuckled O of LOVE and on the knuckled A of HATE.

54
THINGS THE STALKER KNOWS

Stalker knows Bryony's phone number. He knows the series of digits that will give him her voice, as if by magic. But he will wait.

Frog. Tongue. Lily pad.

He says her name: *Bryony.*

People really should be more careful about what they throw away. Stalker's almost annoyed with Bryony, for so carelessly discarding such artefacts, life things. And yet he hankers after them and is grateful for them.

It doesn't take long to paint a picture of her, to feel he knows her – the minutiae of her - as a lover might, as a husband might, as both ought but often don't. He is learning all about Bryony, his red-haired woman, as any self-respecting psycho should. He now knows what pantyliners she uses and at what time of the month she uses them. He knows what painkillers she prefers, but not what pains she suffers. He knows she has a wheat allergy (report from hospital testing) which she sometimes ignores (remains of a wholemeal loaf in the bin). He bullet-points her details in his head. He bullet-points her details in a fresh notebook bought especially for the purpose. He uses red ink. He pastes the documentation salvaged from her bins into a scrapbook. Receipts, train tickets, shopping lists, even junk mail – she mightn't want to join the book club or have new double glazing, so the content is irrelevant, but she has touched these pieces of paper. He wants to kiss her face, snap her fingers off so she cannot run them through her own hair. Only *he* is worthy of that loving but potentially violent act. He wants to break her and put her back together in a different shape. He wants her never to look at anyone but him. She has beautiful eyes. Stalker knows how much Bryony's home is mortgaged for. He knows she cancelled a dentist appointment last month and that her restyled re-coloured enflamed hair cost £105.00 and those new glasses of hers twice that amount. She has an aunt in Canada. She has no one else, it seems, but the three friends. Amy. Christina. Daryl. She is perfect, Bryony. Stalker now knows her email address. Knows exactly where she's @. He says her name again. Bryony. Such a pretty name.

55
WHITE HORSE
Reaper will ride a white stallion. It suited him in the pictures he'd seen. What the hell, you only live once, he thought, and laughed.

56
THINGS ARE CHANGING
The dog hasn't come back. The ugly army has new recruits.
Cupid is in the house of Death. And Death is in an expanded mood.
Things are changing. Things are all turning about.

57
STALKER WORDS HIS WAY IN
The pen is momentarily mightier than any sword. Mightier than scythe or arrow. Stalker writes to Bryony: He even writes her name then tells her, It was love at first sight. The moment I saw you I knew...

58
BLUEPRINT FOR A BLACK NIGHT
Cupid sits in Death's seat at the head of Death's table. He thinks about the boys on the corner, thinks about killing them, and about how he'll do it. Long slow deaths? Or fast? He likes the idea of fast, imagines the scythe's chine slicing through air, hears the whistle the blade will make. Those

heads would look good on spikes. Or rolling... Cupid plans. Cupid plots. Blueprint for a black night. He leaves the door of Death's mansion open...

59
SEND

Stalker presses *SEND*.

60
PARADISE

Death names his white horse Paradise.

61
CUPID VULTURE

The scum soldiers are lined up.

Seven ten pins. Arms folded. Psyching up for the fight. It's not a fair fight.

They site their quarry. A well-dressed male in his forties. They might call him dapper if they knew the word and what it meant. Probably got a wife, kids. They don't care. He's worth kicking in. Why's he out at this time of night, walking, when he could afford a cab? Tight arsed dickhead. He is sidestepping glassy puddles of rain. He doesn't want to stain his shoes.

Cupid flies a vulture circle in the sky, wheeling black against slumberous end-of-evening clouds. Cupid dives. He lands silent, soft and gentle as a gymnast. Falling in behind the scum's victim. Keeping in step, bare foot in rhythm with designer shoe. Nature and artifice in synchronicity. Cupid makes himself seen. Get a load of this. A piece of me.

He's an eyeful all right.

A bouncer in the doorway of a club looks and looks again. It's a boy with wings! He laughs, gives the be-winged thing the thumbs up.

"Nice one, mate. Fancy fucking dress." The bouncer watches as Cupid spreads his span like a cloak behind the victim. Incubus with ugliest intent?

29

Cries from the army:

"Fuck."

"What the..."

"You're shitting me."

They have *seen*.

Cupid shadows the man. He enfolds him, as a mother would a baby to her breast. He feels the body flinch and then relenting in the safety of this brutal salvation, go limp. Cupid flings the body to one side. He isn't interested in him. He'll save him because he wants the army.

Every head. Every single one. Seven heads perched on seven sets of heavy-set shoulders. Fleshy coconut shie.

62
VENUS SHADOW

Venus will make a shadow on the sun.

63
BIG NIGHT, SMALL DOG

The dog is too far from home now to hear Amy calling his name. The night is big and the dog is small. He is lost and panicked by all the noises of the big night and the blinding brightness of the night's lights. Amber ribbons streaming from cars, strobe club signs, green man walking, red man stands stock still. The dog doesn't know the difference between pavement and road. He has a human name and human eyes, but lacks human knowledge. His little metal name tag jingles like a bell about his neck. It has his human name on it, and his human's mobile phone number.

64
CUPID IS WEIGHTLESS

Cupid has risen up; seen scared fish eyes gawping at him, watched coconut heads on strained fat necks follow him as he ascends. He swims above the group of little men. Around and around surveying his prey, disorienting them. He is beautiful, lean, fluid and weightless in the sea of sky. Balletic boy melting one movement into another with fluency of perfect limb and newly stronged muscle, bone and flesh. Even the scythe is now part of him, is part of the dance. They are one, the pretty boy and the wicked toy. Cupid can hear his own blood sing.

65
INSOMNIA

Bryony can't sleep. She fears bad dreams, has been prone to them since childhood, but has no idea that waking reality can and will be more horrifying than any night terror. She gets up. She makes coffee - might as well be fully defiantly awake when sleep proves illusive. She switches on her computer. She checks her emails. There won't be any messages, she thinks. There rarely are. The caffeine makes her jittery. There *is* one. There is *one* message.

66
ANGEL BLADE

The well-dressed man in his forties, the dapper man, has managed to get up, shaking, and stand on his well-shod feet. He steadies himself, checks his pockets to see if his wallet is still there. It is. And his mobile phone, but that isn't working. He staggers through puddles, he doesn't care now about the water damage to his shoes, they cost a fortune but life's worth more than designer shoes, and he thinks, has at least the vaguest notion, that his has just been saved. What the hell just happened to him, what was that all about? He remembers the group of louts on the corner, remembers thinking they looked like trouble, looked like they liked it. And then something else, something indefinable, a *force*, like an angel but fiercer, throwing him out of their path, way out of their path, disorienting him. Sometimes there were documentaries on the TV about unseen hands rescuing people from peril, lifting them with inhuman strength out of the way of danger, catching them as they fell from buildings or cliff-tops, or almost into the maws of wicked machines.

31

But those angels never carried blades. He remembers the blade.

He doesn't look back, he walks, lamely (he hurt his leg in the fall) in the direction of home. Home: where no wife waits. Home: where no children sleep. Home: where only a chocolate-point cat called Vienna waits for him. He'd like a wife, maybe children too, one day. He's just never met the right person. He told Vienna that yesterday. As if she cared.

67
THE REAPER RIDES THE NIGHT

Reaper rides Paradise bareback across the night and experiences lightness of self, alleviation. Elevation.

68
ART OF ARTIFICE

The silk flowers Christina bought herself look strangely real by the dim glow of the clock radio's LED. It is what is called an ungodly hour and she wakes in the night needing to piss and sees them. They'll last forever. The man who'd left her had looked strangely real too. He hadn't lasted a month.

69
TERRIFIED TERRIER

The dog is trotting nervously along the curb, darting back onto the squares of the wet pavement when more zooming streams of roaring cars dash by.

The dapper man, limping, nearly treads on the small dog.

The dog whimpers, crouches.

The man talks to the dog as he talks to his cat. As if it were a person. He reads the dog's I.D. tag, reads the dog's human name and laughs. It's a good name for a dog. Just as it is a good name for a man. It suits this dog. He sees the phone number of the dog's human, but his mobile phone was damaged when the angel threw him so he can't make a call.

It hangs on him, the feeling of responsibility. Someone will be missing this dog. Someone *loves* this dog. Its long salt and peppered hair is wet and tangled, coarse with road dirt. The leathery paw pads are cold and thick with grit. The dog limps. His body shakes.

The dapper man picks him up.

Limping man limps limping dog to the warm safety of his wifeless, childless home. The man sees a thank you in the dog's human eyes. The dog sees salvation in the man's.

It's one hell of a surprise for Vienna.

70
COMING SOON TO A SUN NEAR YOU

Venus plots. Venus plans. Venus the shadow caster.

80
DEAD, STARING, BLIND

The first head comes clean away from the body, a boulder jettisoned to the wet pavement, landing with a thud, an unreal sound-effect thump, a radio drama sound. Lifeless fish eyes stare blind. There's more expression in them dead than when they were alive. Fear, fixed. The sorrowless inked tear obscured by blood.

One down. Six to go.

The six wail and cling to each other, they try at first to run, but Cupid's atramentous shadow is cast across them like a net. They cannot move. There is no escape. Floundering fish trawled and trapped. The blood runs black in the rain: from the severed head, and from the headless body lying feet away.

Cupid shakes with boyish excitement. He flexes his wings. Black blood drips from oil-black blade.

81
SENT, RECEIVED

It was love at first sight. The moment I saw you I knew...

82
CELESTIAL SCHEDULE
On June 8th 2004 Venus will mark the sun.

83
1 DOWN, 6 TO GO
The fat boys scream and whimper like girls.

84
WOMAN FRUIT
Daryl plans the feast for Venus day. She imagines her table laden with spreads of Arcimboldoesque fruit. Pomegranates with their engorged lickable clitoral seeds. Apples, sliced through and ripening to brown, the sweet sugared shape and honeyed curve of a woman's core imprinted there – like the name of a seaside town through a stick of rock.

85
GRANTED WISH
Bryony will read the email over and over in the night. She'll keep coming back to it. She won't quite believe it. It's creepy, and yet it will make her feel mysterious, desirable, somehow elevated. A secret admirer. And... love at first sight. Who can it be? Someone she knows?

One wish granted. Should she reply? One wish granted. Love at first sight.

86
CAT AND DOG
The dapper man introduces the dog to his cat, Vienna. "This is Bill," he says. "Say hello, Bill. Bill. Vienna. Vienna. Bill." The animals stare at each other, like newly-acquainted children, shy and reluctant to make friends.

The man seeks out an old bowl in a cupboard. He puts water down for Bill. He dries Bill's tangled wet coat with an old towel. He pats him. "Good boy." He phones the number on Bill's ID tag.

"*Hello?* Hello. I'm… Oh, you don't know me… It's, I'm sorry, it's terribly late. I, I expect you've been worried. I'm… I'll start again… It's Will… I mean Bill, it's about Bill."

The man talks to animals as if they were people. He talks to people with difficulty, when he has to talk to them at all.

87
HATE FOLLOWS LOVE

The blade cuts clean through one thick gristly wrist. And LOVE falls to the wet pavement. The blade cuts clean through the other wrist. HATE follows LOVE. Cupid watches the minutes of the man tick away. He's still standing, faltering on his feet. Look, no hands! All the bravado is bleeding out of his veins. He curls to the pavement like an oversized foetus. He dies silently. The other five do all his screaming for him. They scream for themselves. They cannot escape Cupid's net. Cupid hacks the sorry head from Mr LOVE-HATE's corpse and bowls it along the pavement, watches it land next to Pierrot's boulder. Who's next? Cupid wipes the bloodied blade of his tool on one caliginous wing. Shakes himself off like a preening bird and assesses his prey. Checks the damage he's done.

They stand, backs against the wall of a betting shop.

Cupid rises up, to swim the sky again. Cupid sings. A diabolical adaptation of a nursery rhyme song in a voice so angelic he almost weeps, like he is remembering who once he was, what he had been, before this, before his transmogrification. *Five foul fiends up against the wall.* The octaves getting higher and higher, as he does. *Five foul fiends up against the wall. And if one foul fiend should accidentally fall…*

88
THE REAPER FLASHES A
FLASH SMILE AT EARTH

Reaper urges Paradise on through the night, cracks an imaginary whip across the creature's muscled haunches, applies pressure with his well-turned heels against the animal's shimmering silver flanks. The Reaper flashes a flash smile at Earth, and at the planets, and at all the stars the wishful wakeful are wishing on. He waves to Venus.

Planet of Love.

His new Sun. He's forgotten Venus is Cupid's mother's name. The name means nothing much to him nor to the cherub anymore.

He waves with a flourish.

He sings out to Venus:

"You are my sunshine, my only sunshine."

He's just being jolly, there's nothing in it.

99
LAKE BECOMES OCEAN

Amy hears her mobile phone ringing. She hears a man's voice. Maybe the line is bad. Nothing's making sense. Then...

"It's about Bill."

Amy can hear herself sobbing. Amy can still hear the man's voice, but is afraid to listen to what he has to say, what he's trying to say. Her sobs swamp the sounds of him.

"It's about Bill."

She really *loves* that dog. Amy is starting to *feel.* Amy *is* feeling.

Bryony is writing an email and drinking more coffee. She's jittering.

Christina puts on an old movie, a love story. Black and white. Mollusced lovers whose kisses never miss.

Daryl is dreaming of her lover. Dreaming that they are together but apart, reaching toward one another across a silvered stream, hands outstretched, trying to fit their blue puzzle pieces together... but something is wrong and the pieces won't join. And the silvered stream becomes a silvery lake and then an ocean, silver still but vast. Uncrossable?

Uncrossable.

There is a bridge but it breaks when the stream becomes a lake and the lake swells to an ocean. And she is there,

Daryl, she can see herself – nacreous, all the colours of the spectrum of her soul made somehow subtle and metallic in the gown she wears.

The Stalker is abed, a pair of Bryony's discarded/salvaged tights pulled taut – a meshed mask - against his mouth, against his nose. He can hardly breathe and yet he feels he has only just learned to. He is only three or four expert jerks of the wrist away from ecstasy, and from hollow guilt and shame and messes that must be wiped away and not spoken of.

Bryony, what's there of her in the lycra, smells of oats and, strangely, of his mother. He doesn't want to think of his mother. Naughty boy. Dirty boy. Bad boy.

Still five to kill. Cupid comes down from the skies, sharps his blade on the curb and kills one - Scythe blade through the heart... then:

Two - Scythe chine across the back of the head.

Three - The hook of the tool swung upward between the legs, splitting, cross-sectioning the body with the accuracy of a surgeon.

Four - Same again. A vertical slicing. He falls in half. Left and right of torso felled like trees to the pavement. Cupid likes that.

Five – In half again, but this time the other way, horizontal. It's an action so swiftly and cleanly executed that the severed torso sits awhile atop the lower half of the body before slowly falling to one side and thudding down, butcher's shop carcass. The legs follow.

Cupid takes a memento from each of the dead:

- a set of keys
- a finger
- a sovereign ring
- an unticking fake designer watch with a smashed in face

- a belcher chain
- a tooth of gold
- a shin bone sharp as a tusk – human ivory.

These grim bloodspattered trophies he puts into the discarded carrier that still stinks of kebab. It's a party bag. He's had such fun.

Cupid is pleased with his work. So too is the Reaper. Love's gotten hold of him. Love is the new Death.

100
THINGS HAVE CHANGED

Things have changed. Things have turned about.

INTERLUDE

THE FOUR WOMEN

AMY

There is no such thing as Love, Amy, the first woman, said. She claimed she'd never been in it. She'd never been in the sea but she knew it existed, she'd seen it and seen others in the summers of their lives laughing and diving down into it, waiting for the splash, plunging in, despite the perils of filth and fearsome beasts. But with Love it was different. She'd never seen anyone in it. She'd never learned to swim and feared drowning.

Prologue – Book 1- Cupid's Scythe (Grim's Bow)

Amy claimed never to have believed in love, or in God. "I've seen no proof of either," she said. She was born, she thought, to be a spinster type and once this thought had taken hold she moulded her life and her self to fit the stereotype. It was easier that way. No other person to consider, man or woman...

But Amy had loved once. A boy with a girl's face. William. It was a long time ago. Her parents disapproved and feared for her. She was too young; the boy with the girl's face was too young. There were dangers, unwanted children, disease, shame. What would they say in church if those sorts of rumours got passed around the congregation like a collection box? They said God would condemn her. You are fifteen years old, young lady, said her father, in voice that suggested he thought he *was* God or was speaking for him.

The subject of God was raised like a threat at the table during family dinners. Her father spoke constantly of God's love while her mother twitched and shifted in her seat. For all this talk of love there was little joy. And what God in his right mind, what God with any benevolence would want to stop a girl loving a boy with a girl's face?

She decided not to believe anything.

But now she felt different. She felt, she imagined, more like Bryony and Daryl and Christina did. They talked about sex and love constantly; she had lately begun to think about these things too. She wondered suddenly why these three women were friends with her at all, given their differences. It didn't occur to her that they'd ever felt sorry for her, or even that such sympathy, such consideration, their determination to include her in things, to embrace her, were forms of love. It had struck her that she loved that poor little lost dog very much indeed. Yes, she really did love that dog. Dog with human eyes. Bill.

She didn't know how she was going to thank the man who was bringing Bill home today, but she'd think of something. And then, because she was not fully in charge of her own destiny, she would do something completely out of the ordinary, because something completely out of the ordinary would happen.

Reaper was watching, Reaper was loving this. He was a clever fucker, though he said so himself.

BRYONY

I believe in Love at first sight, said the second woman, Bryony, her wantful eye on the waiter, her hopeful heart swelling her breast. She looked about the restaurant for Cupid. He was not there. It's not like in the movies, she thought, as imagined arrows missed her. Again.

Prologue – Book 1- Cupid's Scythe (Grim's Bow)

Bryony is a romantic. She always has been. Not for her the organised box-ticking type of relationship that a heartless statistic-based computer program recommends. Not for her just any type of love. She wants the overblown fantasy; she wants to be Cinderella, Sleeping Beauty. She wants love at first sight. If it happens, with their eyes meeting across a proverbially crowded room, all the better. She likes a cliché, Bryony.

And…

CHRISTINA

The third woman, Christina, said, *Love should be forever.* She was steeped in three-weeks' worth of ardour from a man who would be gone away the next day. Forever. Love came and stayed awhile, but would not outstay its welcome. The three-week man had expensive tickets to Somewhere in the pocket of his expensive jacket. He would leave a note on her bed, and a bunch of loud afterthought flowers in unthoughtful colours. £4.99.

Prologue – Book 1- Cupid's Scythe (Grim's Bow)

C hristina chooses not to remember her past.

DARYL

No one said Love was a sickness. No one said it was a disease or a madness. Not even Daryl, the fourth woman, and she knew well enough that it was an incurable condition. She knew it could send you crazy. She knew too that it could kill. Love, she claimed, is the thing that makes you afraid of death, your lover's and your own. She sipped her wine. She said, You're unlikely to die together. One of you must be left behind. There are natural, if unfair, orders of things.

Prologue – Book 1- Cupid's Scythe (Grim's Bow)

Daryl had been married once, years ago, to man she had not loved. On her wedding day she felt analytical, rather than emotional. Was she doing the right thing? The fact that she even had to ask meant that she wasn't. She did not recognise him, this man she had agreed to marry: he had had his wild hair cut the day before (an act she had not known he was planning) and he looked unfamiliar, scrubbed and neat; a defendant going to court, a boy, all apple-shiny-clean on his first day at school, like he wanted to put across a him that was not him, a better him, a more responsible him.

Later, when she looked at the wedding photographs (this was before they had been torn up and thrown away) she realised that she too seemed unlike herself, she was a cynical stranger in a Cinderella gown, her hair upswept in accordance with her mother's wishes for a classic look, her lips varnished to a high gloss, her smile frozen. In one picture she was sitting by her groom's side, her left hand cradled like a frail newborn in the lap of her right, a gently sad nursing gesture, as if the weight of the duties of matrimony lay in that single gold band on the finger of her left hand and caused her pain.

Pretty little shackle gleaming on her finger, *tight* on her finger. The ring had never fitted. There'd been a problem at the jewellers and so she'd had to make do with one that was a half size too small. Now, when she looked back she thought that meant something, that it was an omen.

They were married thirteen years. For the first nine they lived together in a dilapidated Victorian terraced house that was too large to heat and yet too small to accommodate all their misgivings. The house itself, with its peeling paintwork and crumbling ceiling roses would have made an ideal backdrop, had she and he been a romantic couple, but they were not and the building's faults, endearing maybe if viewed through the eyes of true lovers, seemed only to reflect the deterioration of their relationship, and moreover the crumbling state of Daryl's husband's mind. And so they played out their first acts, their unrehearsed scenes and took their final curtain calls on this faded and elegant stage: am-dram newbies flung headfirst into Shakespeare. Their battles raged and their neighbours on either side (happier more established people, unaccustomed to conflict) complained - to the various authorities who would listen but not actually do anything.

Daryl knew Love could send you crazy, so too the lack of it. The tenth year was peaceful, at least for Daryl. She used to visit her husband on Wednesdays and Saturdays, coming away with the stench of antiseptic and others' madnesses in her nostrils. Coming home to the dilapidated terraced house where she'd sigh her sighs of relief in its now quiet rooms and bathe to wash away the day and sleep safely. Her husband slept safely too, curved like a pupae in his madman's bed, his dulled head lolling chestward, his arms wrapped like straight-jacket straps around his torso.

By the end of the eleventh year she stopped visiting. But the stink of insanity remained in her, haunted her, an olfactory memory.

Daryl knew Love could send a person crazy. And sometimes they stayed that way. The divorce finalised almost exactly thirteen years after the day she had married - all her doing, there were grounds enough, the solicitor said. She swore then that she'd never marry again, but now she longs to however unconventional it would seem.

She can still smell madness, can smell it now, but she doesn't know if it is a fresh madness all her own or just the faint echoing aroma of what has gone before. She suspects it is her own un-solid state she is detecting. Love, after all, *can* send you crazy, this she knows and she is irrevocably in it. LOVE.

LOVE, it can be etched, scrawled in blueish black, across the knuckles of a thug. It can be present, like a watermark, through your soul. It can be many things, mostly indescribable.

CUPID'S SCYTHE
(GRIM'S BOW)

BOOK II

CUPID'S SCYTHE

(GRIM'S BOW)

BOOK II

**"They that love beyond the world
cannot be separated by it.
Death cannot kill what never dies."**

William Penn

1
THINGS HAVE CHANGED

Things have turned about.
Things have changed.
Look…

2
YOU CAN BUY ANYTHING ONLINE

Stalker orders a set of ophthalmic surgical speculums online, not up to the minute kit, these are vintage, rusted.

The description reads: *Please note: Not suitable for medical use but ideal for the enthusiast or collector.* It's ninety-five quid well spent.

3
CUPID SLEEPS

Now the seven are slain Cupid sleeps the heavy sleep of the dead in Death's cold bed.

It's a good number 7 – shaped like a scythe, *the* scythe, *his* scythe, his favourite toy.

Ah, bless. Little man has had a busy day.

4
LOVE IS GOOD FOR YOU

Love is good for you, muses the Reaper. He's in love with the concept of Love, he's in love with the idea of being it and being in it, and it's making him feel... what? Alive? Young? Warm inside. Fucking big softy.

5
DELUSION

Christina convinces herself that the fake flowers are real, and that they'll last forever. Fool. Not all is fair in love...

6
8TH JUNE 2004 IS COMING

Nearly party time, my treasure, writes Daryl in an email to her lover. She doesn't receive a reply instantly, but sometimes that happens. She'll give it an hour or so, a few hours, a day maybe. There are other commitments. She's not going to let it worry her. (She *is* going to let it worry her.) Not all is fair in love...

7
LOVE AT FIRST SIGHT

Bryony keeps reading the email from her mystery admirer: *It was love at first sight.* She sighs. It's just what she wished for. She'll wish she'd been more careful about what she'd wished for one day. And that day is coming soon. Not all is fair in love...

8
BILL

The man is going to take Bill home to Amy. Limping down streets he doesn't usually go down. Past greengrocers and halal shops. He buys the dog a lead from the pet shop the dog had once been the doggy in the window of. Now they can limp together. Slowly does it. Small steps. No giant leaps for man or dogkind.

9
VENUS WILL SHOW HER SHADOW

Not long now.

10
DEATH'S BED

Cupid in repose might appear more innocent than he really is, the wicked often do and his features are still pretty-boyish, lean, androgynous even, but his cherubic face is a burnished mask of devil blood.

11
ROSES ARE RED

The ungrimmed elegant Reaper sits atop a refuse bin in an alleyway, scattering red rose petals amongst the overspilled stinkpile of refuse. He produces elaborate bouquets from the air with a magician's sweeping slighting hand, and from behind his own ear, from out of nowhere.

12
DARYL WAITS

When a long hour has passed Daryl tells herself she'll wait another. Still nothing from her lover.

Not all is fair...

XIII
HOW LONG IS FOREVER?

Christina wonders how long forever is. She could wonder this for ever.

Not all is fair...

14
KILLER SLUMBER

Cupid in slumber. Here sleeps a killer in Death's wormed four poster bed. Here sleeps a vengeful daemon, a winged beast, a savage Pterodactylus resurrected. Impious phoenix-boy risen from the bone dust ashes of Death's mansion.

Fireless. Fearless.

15
ROSES AGAIN

The man walks slowly down an alleyway with the slow walking dog. Rose petals stick to his shoes and to the dog's bristly fur and leathery paw pads. The Reaper caresses the air with his gloved hands: a rose bush grows from the unfertile pile of debris. The bush is thorny, and in bud. As it blooms the thorns wilt and drip like tears down the stems.

16
THE MISADVENTUROUS
DEATHS OF THE SEVEN DEAD

The police will write the deaths of the seven off as misadventure. Whoever is responsible for the cull of the notorious vermin has done society a good turn. Whoever loses the case files, and what little evidence there is, will have done society a good turn too.

17
CUPID DREAMS

Cupid dreams of killing again. Not of killing with his own hands, this time he wants to watch as another kills at his command. That's true power. Hands off.

18
EYE WITNESS

They're supposed to be looking for a lad who was out in fancy dress the night of the killings. The bouncer from the nearby club (the only eye witness to have come forward) says he saw someone, some *thing*. "Like an angel,' he says. "It was a thing like a fuckin' angel with a devil's eyes."

19
STORMSTREAM

Reaper blows a kiss from his white-gloved palm and makes a breeze that carries an everlasting stormstream of petals down the alleyway, and out ... up up up above the world. This bloodbird flock is seen from below as a shapeshifting swarm: an-apple-becomes-a-snake...

20
DON'T SEEK AND YE SHAN'T FIND

They won't bother searching for the boy who's being dubbed the 'Angel of Death'. And even if they did, would they find Cupid? Would they see Cupid? Cupid is only seen if he wants to be seen. No one will find him. No one really cares whose hands are stained with the blood of the seven dead.

21
SHAPES SHIFT

And the snake...
   becomes-a-man...

22
GOOD MOURNING

Thin-mouthed girls line the scene-of-slaughter pavements with soft toys and dying flowers, inappropriate tributes stolen respectively from the cribs of babies and the graves of the more deserving. They light candles and leave misspelled notes of misplaced sympathy. *"u will be mist" "forevva in are hearts"* Their tears are real, their reasons are varied. They didn't know the dead pre-death but it's *well* good mourning them.

23
SHIFTING SHAPES

And the man...
   becomes-a-woman...

24
WHAT THE PAPERS SAY

The papers are calling the seven dead The Angel's Seven. This is their fifteen minutes. The title elevates them, somewhat. Give it a little while and some stick-legged, bristle-chinned Indie trio will take the title as their band name and launch a so-called seminal album of the same name. In the name of shame, this is how the world works.

25
SHAPES RESHAPE

And the woman…

becomes a woman and a man…

26
THE NAMES OF THE SLAIN

And the names of the slain shall become known, spoken, written. The names of the slain shall become pub quiz answers. TV ghost hunters will hunt the houses they once lived in for hauntings. They'll be mentioned in books of unsolved crimes.

27
CULT

In a movie that will quickly be known as cultish, the seven dead will be played by actors far too human and appealing to accurately represent what the dismal reality of them was.

28
ICONS

And years on the seven faces of The Angel's Seven will be shoddily screen-printed Warhol style on t-shirts and tote bags worn and carried by Camden girls who weren't even born in 2004. Every seven years people will remember they forgot to remember them and some fresh-out-of-uni upstart with a Desmond in Watching Telly will make a documentary – all hand held cameras and shifty angles – about the murdered. There might even be a penny to be made with a line of commemorative mugs with the seven dead's mugs on them some day.

The englamourment, the glorification, the making saints of sinners, deification of the dead - just for being dead.

But death is no big deal; it's as easy as 1, 2, 3. It's as easy as A, B, C. Ask Cupid.

29
GOOGLED

The Reaper Googles himself. It's still the old him popping up in search results. It's a shame, he thinks. After all, a man can change. He's got a new mythology now. He's reinvented himself. He's transformed. He doesn't want to be known as the Reaper anymore. He doesn't see himself as Death. Lots of things have changed, things have all turned about.

30
SHAPE ON SHAPE

And the woman and the man...
become one. One.

31
CUNT

Cupid wishes there was more media coverage of his work, a more faithful depiction of his deathly debut. He likes being called the Angel of Death but he resents that it's the mainly the slain that make the headlines, not the slayer. The world is a wrong place. It's not right. None of this Angel's Seven soundbiting bullshit for Cupid. Why big up the small fry? Even numbering them 1-7 seems somehow too respectful. He has his own special name for each of the seven:

1.   Cunt
2.   Cunt
3.   Cunt
4.   Cunt
5.   Cunt
6.   Cunt

And finally, his favourite...

7.   Cunt

Cupid likes swearing. It makes him feel big. What would his mother say?

Fuck her.

He's the Angel of Death, what's she gonna do? Ground him?

32
VENUS
Soon Venus, shady sister.

33
SHAPE FROM SHAPE ON SHAPE
And the One blooms into a baby which shift-shows all of its lifecycle across the clouds in seconds.

The petals spread, converge and hang heavy in place of the sun for a while. And then, just as the man with the dog looks up to check, for no reason at all, if rain might be coming, the petals form a simple symbol; a heart shape that rose tints the world.

A Valentine heart shape.

34
SPEAK NOT ILL OF THE DEAD
The Angel's Seven bandwagon is in town. A grandmother of one of the dead talks to a newbie hack from the local paper.

"He was a lovely boy, such a sunny little lad, all smiles," she says.

"Fuck off," says Cupid.

35
SOFT
"Take that darling little doggy home," whispers the Reaper.

Told you he was a fucking softy.

It's hearts and flowers and puppies all day long with him.

36
THE LITTLE KING OF KILL

A girl says she was the girlfriend of one of the dead. She tells a blonde woman on daytime television: "We was going to get married. He was the love of my life. We was really close."

"Oh *was* you?" spits Cupid. "Love of your life? Ha ha fuck fucking ha! It wasn't you he was sticking his prick in the night I killed him. Fuck off. Don't talk to me about love."

Ah, Cupid. Ah, Love. The boy was once the prince of that pretty passion. Now he's the little King of Kill.

37
WILLIAM

Bill jumps up at Amy. Amy really loves this dog but, much as she's been longing for him to come home she can't look at him, can't acknowledge him. She's frozen in a moment she'll remember forever, looking at a face she's never forgotten.

"*William?*" asks Amy.

Not all is fair in love... but just sometimes *some* things are.

Watch...

38
STALKER'S GIFT TO HIMSELF

A parcel arrives. The ophthalmic speculums. *Not suitable for medical use but ideal for the ~~enthusiast or collector~~ weirdo.*

"Happy birthday to me, happy birthday to me, happy birthday dear *me-eee*, happy birthday to me," sings the Stalker.

He sings out of tune, and it's not his birthday. He doesn't know when his birthday is. Not officially. Who cares? He's shopping online again. There are other things he needs.

39
A MOTHER'S LOSS - A MOTHER'S GAIN

One of the motherfuckers' mothers is calling for the evil killer to be tracked down and brought to justice. She's interviewed in a women's magazine. Double page spread of contrived heartache and snapshots of the thug as a baby – a slug in a nappy, and as a schoolboy - a pig in a blazer and… thank you *very much* for the £2,000, I'm off to Spain. It's what her Ricky would have wanted.

Costa del Sol. Cost of the soul.

"Fuck the almighty fuck of fucks *off*," says Cupid, simply because he likes saying fuck.

40
THE SMALL AND QUIET DEATH
OF CUT FLOWERS LEAVES A SCENT

William, boy with a girl's face; now a man with a man's face.

William and Bill tread rose petals onto Amy's hall floor.

Even the small and quiet death of cut flowers leaves a scent.

Not all things are fair in love, but some things, *sometimes* thankfully, *are*.

The Reaper watches. He sheds a little tear. It's all very moving, this love lark. Now, what's he going to do about Christina? Will he get to her before Cupid does?

41
THE SEVEN ANGELS

People are starting to call the Angel's Seven the Seven Angels. Cupid is not happy. Why do people get things so wrong? What's the matter with them? Why do they, unthinking, so willingly worship the unworthy? This is *his* apocalypse, his maiden voyage of murder and he doesn't want that overlooked. People are such idiots. They can't correctly read things that are written down, and they can't read the unwritten because they don't know it's there. They know nothing of angels.

42
WHEN LOVE TURNS TO WAR

Daryl checks her emails, checks her mobile phone for texts, missed calls. Nothing. Not all is fair in love and war. Not all is fair when love turns to war, and that it can quickly do, when vengeful scythe replaces well-intentioned arrow, when the words of the Book of Love are rewritten in blood in a grimoire, and the Book of the Dead has died. Things are all turned about. Things are changed. There's a shadow coming.

43
HOW TO SAFELY LOOK AT VENUS

"The transit of the planet Venus is an extraordinary and arresting phenomenon you simply won't want to miss - however you must observe safety guidelines. Don't let the mandatory warnings alarm you! You can experience the transit of Venus in safety, but it is imperative that you protect your eyes at all times with the use of proper solar filters. NEVER stare continuously at the sun. Take regular breaks and give your eyes a rest! And remember, sunglasses don't offer sufficient protection to the eyes."

44
THANK YOU

"Thank you for bringing Bill home," says Amy.
"It was really nothing," says William.

45
REAPER GETS A TATTOO

Reaper gets a tattoo. A heart above his heart, a heart so red and vivid it almost appears to dance against the newly heard and newly felt offbeat of his own - a heart sashed with the word LOVE across it.

46
STALKER PAYS THROUGH
THE NOSE FOR EYE DROPS

You really can get anything online these days. The Stalker orders *tropicamide* and *phenylephrine*, jewellers' forceps (tweezers), anaesthetising drops for the eyes, sunglasses. Sod the extra expense; he opts for next day delivery. She's worth it.

He says her name.

Bryony.

It's misleading how untainted the Stalker seems, mythical, godlike almost with that golden crown of hair.

He wonders if he's Bryony's type, not that it matters.

He wonders if she even has a type.

He wonders if she prefers blonds.

He knows so much about her and yet knows nothing.

What he learns of her he learns from careful analysis and the fanatical cataloguing of the things she throws away.

He knows what he knows from watching her.

He knows nothing of her heart. Even if he did, he wouldn't empathise. He wouldn't empathise simply because he can't, the psycho.

47
THE KISS

There's an email from Daryl's lover. It's brief. It lacks feeling.

It says: See you on Venus day. x

That's it. Just that. Just one kiss. The kiss looks like a crossing-out of something, the opposite of a tick in a box, a negative. Something is wrong. Daryl can feel it. It's not right. Not all in love or war is fair…

48
VENUS

She's coming.

49
UNDRESSED TO KILL

Cupid heads out at night. He's got thick leather bands on his wrists, skull rings on his fingers and…why wear one belt when one can wear five? His are all black, all leather, studded, slung about his slender jutting pelvis like holsters, strapping down his seditious virgin cock. From these restraints hang his keepsakes from the kill: The set of keys, the severed finger, the garish sovereign ring of lightweight gold, the unticking fake designer watch with its smashed face, the belcher chain, the tooth of gold, the human ivory shin bone. You might say he's dressed to kill, but he's naked except for the belts, the wrist bands, and an almighty pair of fuck off *New Rock* boots. *Undressed to kill?* Cupid won't kill again just yet. Not yet.

50
CHRISTINA

You think Reaper and Cupid have forgotten Christina? Wrong.

51
THE LAMP BENEATH WHICH
THE PREY HAD LURKED

Cupid, unseen at the scene of the crime, flies up, hovers, spins and jabs his long lean-muscled leg out, kicks the street lamp under which his prey had lurked, boots out the light with his new studded boots, he wants to darken the darkness of the death scene, dark it one shade darker than hell, one shade darker than early mourning. Blackened black could be the new black.

People say killers always return to the scenes of their crimes. Cupid has. But he is only seen if he wants to be seen. He doesn't want to be seen. Not yet. But he'll want to show off those boots sometime soon. Oh the vanity, and... he wants to get himself fucked. He can smell sex. His own.

52
CHRISTINA

Christina.

You still think Reaper and Cupid have forgotten her? Wrong. She's forgotten herself, that's all. You'll never guess who Cupid wants to fuck.

53
REAPER'S NEVER BEEN KISSED

The Reaper's had his hair cut. It's a short sharp look, razored neatly at the sideburns. He can get away with it with that bone structure. He's looking very distinguished, silvered grey at the temples but the face is both mature and youthful. He's an odd mix. His now fleshed skull is abloom with life - high cheekbones, strong jaw, deep set blue eyes. That was unexpected. Even he'd expected them to be black. But he's not Death anymore; this is how he's evolved into his new role. He is no longer darkness. Those eyes are as blue as a storm in an ocean, shaded by the carved blade of his brow. He knows he's damned handsome. He licks his lips, runs his tongue over his strong white teeth. He wonders what it might be like to kiss someone, and to be kissed. Reaper has never been kissed. He's dispensed with the moustache now; he cut himself doing so, he who was once so good with a scythe can't even handle a razor now.

He's like every man, slicing himself to bits in the morning, an attempt to look cleaner, less like a hairy horny wantfilled animal. Less like the beast he is. Smooth.

54
BREATHE

BREATHE.
    Can't?
    Try.
    Yeah, he's hot, isn't he? The Reaper.

55
RITUAL

When the *tropicamide* and *phenylephrine* arrive the Stalker decants both into decorative bottles. There's still the vintage bouquet of *Grès'* smokey *Cabochard* in one and *Givenchy's* amber scented *L'Interdit*, in the other. He's not a romantic but ritual is important to him. He's washed the bottles one hundred times over, but they still maintain the now aged and cloying scent of his mother. These are perfumes that evoke a sense of longing in him, a guilty discordant want. Oedipus.

56
EIGHTY-FOUR INCHES OF PURE HIM

The new heart tattoo over the Reaper's heart feels like it has a quickening beat all its own. He takes a shower. It's what people do, and he wants to be like 'people'. He wants to be like a man. Seven feet of pure man.

"That's eighty-four inches of pure *Me*," says the Reaper looking at his naked self in a full length mirror.

And fourteen inches of cock, when he's at rest.

He strokes himself with his magician's hand. Instant magic in a deft movement. "Call that *sixteen* inches," he says, "for now at least." He winks at his reflection.

He wants to be like a real man.

Only a real woman can make him feel like a real man.

So…

Ready, ladies?

Reaper has never been kissed.

You'll never guess who Reaper wants to kiss.

57
CHRISTINA

See? Told you Reaper and Cupid hadn't forgotten Christina.

58
SHE'S COMING

Venus. She's coming. June brides tan their hides. The sun claims golden dominion over the long days.

59
THE SMITHS

"You still like the Smiths, then?" says Amy to William. They've been catching up over coffee, revisiting their old selves, introducing their new selves. It's been a long time. Bill is attention seeking, chewing at William's trouser leg, barking in a new voice.

"Come to daddy," says William, picking Bill up.

"Wine?" asks Amy.

Not all is fair in love and war but just sometimes some things are. And the fair things seem to be moving fast here, in this house that smells of cut flowers and dog biscuits. The wine will fuel this fast burning fire.

60
TRIBUTE ACTS

The bouncer of the club has gained minor celebrity status. Girls hang on his every word, they hang on his arm, they suck his cock – door work's never been so much fun. Camp boys had taken to dressing as the Angel of Death to go clubbing. Ten wannabes came in one night. Not one of them had Cupid's raw sinewed wickedness. Their fancy dress wings were too frail for flight, but they achieved a certain sexy appeal with their outfits, reminiscent of feral Peter Pans. Girls liked it. Boys liked it too. Women liked it, and men. The manager of the club liked it too; saw a profit to be made. Theme nights always went down well with the freaks. He'd had some flyers printed up.

61
CHRISTINA

Oh Christina. Started giving the fake flowers real fresh water, have we? That's sad. Feel alone? Feel like no one knows you exist? That's sad too. Still wondering how long forever is?

But things have changed, things have all turned about. Can't you feel it? Why can't you feel it? Don't you know what's coming?

62
COMING

Venus is coming.

63
CUMMING

Amy is cumming. William is cumming.

Reaper rubs his hands together. This is all his doing. He's very proud. He's watched them kissing, watched them making love. He's watched them sweetly whisper nothings into each others' ears.

Reaper has never been kissed. He wants to kiss and be kissed.

64
AND SOME SHALL CRY

Even with the lamp kicked out the scene of the crime is still well lit and not as dark as Cupid would like it what with the nearby club's garish strobes and neons and the zooming streams of cars on the road.

But wait, what's this? Cupid spies a poster framed and illuminated in the club's doorway. *Angel of Death Theme Night!* Shit. Some pouty boy model stands, lithe legs apart, spangled pants, a set of wings on elastic strapped to his shoulders – he's holding a plastic joke shop scythe. "Ha ha ha!" Cupid laughs at the joke even though it's not funny and not even meant to be a joke.

"Wait til they see the actual thing. My beautiful blade, my real rod, my sexy staff, my untumbling tower, my weapon of war, my tremendous tool." His cock strains against his belts, wetting the rough suede of them with pre-cum. "Wait til they see the *real me*," says Cupid, laughing his ungodly laugh. "These tribute acts got nothing on me."

It's Cupid's party, and he'll make them cry if he wants to, and he wants to.

And some shall cry for fear. And some shall cry for the beauty of this beast shall make them cry. And some shall cry with envy. And some shall cry and beg for more.

And one will cry for it to stop. STOP. Crying is not a safeword.

65
THE SHADOW OF SOON AND
LOVE'S LITTLE DEATH

Venus is coming.

Amy and William are cumming together, right now.

66
FLOWERS

The Reaper wonders if he should take flowers to Christina. He knows she likes them and he's seen men do that in those romantic old movies she watches, the movies that make her cry. But she's got flowers, he's seen that too, seen her giving them fresh water. No, he won't take flowers.

He gives his delicate bow and exquisite arrow a little wipe over. As far as he can tell women don't like dirt and dust. He doesn't really know what women like but he thinks that attention to cleanliness and a big penis would stand any man in fairly good stead. He's in with as good a chance as any then, surely.

Mmm. Kissing must feel wonderful, thinks the Reaper.

67
COMING – CUM – NOT COMING

Venus, she's coming.

Amy and William have cum. Daryl's lover isn't coming. Daryl doesn't know this yet.

68
NOT ALL IS FAIR IN LOVE AND WAR

Not all is fair in love and war. Sorry, it just isn't.

69
AMY AND WILLIAM

"Morrissey's almost too vegetarian now, isn't he?" says William. Amy laughs. She's cooking steak for them, they're drinking more wine. There'll be a little bit of meat left over for Bill. William's phoned a neighbour, asked them to put food and water down for Vienna.

70
THAT SINGLE X

What is customary? Three kisses? Two? Daryl thinks one seems so spare, so meaningless.

1 x X

X

Ex.

The X, that kiss, might as well be shaped like boot, a shoulder (a cold one) or an elbow.

Love can drive you mad. Daryl knows this. Loss of it can drive you madder. She knows this too.

Descending.

71
BLADE

"No blades, mate," says the bouncer to Cupid. He doesn't recognise him, doesn't register him as standing out amongst the sea of glittery imitators queuing to gain entry into the club. He's on a high himself, he's been sucked off, puffed up and is self obsessed and Cupid's changed, grown, darkened of aspect, matured. Angel of Death theme night's turning out to be very camp. There's even going to be a prize for the best outfit. Let the best man win.

Cupid points to a sparkly boy with a plastic scythe. "*He's* got a blade," he says, in a petulant schoolboy's voice to the bouncer. "Not fair if you let him in and not me."

"Yeah, but look at it," says the bouncer, "his is plastic, a *KFC* spork's more menacing to be fair. Sorry pal, you can't bring yours in here, classified as a dangerous weapon that is."

Cupid's scythe is a part of him. He's going nowhere without it. Cupid is only seen if he wants to be seen.

"Where the fuck's he gone?" says the bouncer, looking around for Cupid.

Cupid's inside now.

72
HE MAKES HER SHIVER

Christina's surprised when the doorbell rings. She's not expecting anyone. She never is, but especially not at this time of night, not after dark. She looks out of the window, there's a man there, a really tall man.

He's not holding a clipboard or a copy of the *Watchtower*. That's all right then.

Oh, but he's *so* tall, *so* handsome... it makes her shiver. She feels like she knows him. *He* makes her feel like she knows him.

He's the sort of stranger you can't say no to.

73
KILLER, DANCER, FUCKER

Cupid's scythe was built for the seven foot Reaper. It stands over nine feet tall. He could take the club's lights out with one swing of it if he wanted to; rotate its blade above the fluid mass of dry humping bodies on the dance floor and smash all the rainbow lights.

The lookalikes' wings are already tattered, shedding feathers in the air, dripping and drooping with sweat. His own are pristine tonight, petrol-black and sheened, oiled with the sap of his new masculine energy; he's past what was a rapid onset version of puberty and is fully matured now, at least physically. His hair is as white as black isn't and spiked like a crown of icicle thorns about his head.

The music is loud, everyone is dancing. People are weird. The way they move, it's weird. Cupid feels like dancing. He's never done it before. So many new things to try. He's tried killing, liked it. He hopes dancing is as much fun, and that fucking will be too.

74
REAPER'S FIRST KISS

Kissing Christina was like coming home, not home to the bone dust floor mansion that had once been his place of restful unrest, not home to the familiar discomfort of his wormed four poster bed in his bone cathedral abode. Not home to any cradle of cobwebs, nor to the nurturing amniotic safety of a mother's warm wet red womb. He had no mother. The Death that he once was was never born of the life of any real woman.

75
LORD OF THE DANCE
Cupid's slender hips are moving; slowly at first, gently gyrating to the music's beat. His foot taps. He wedges the scythe's handle between his legs, freeing his hands so he can clap them.

CLAP-CLAP!

Cupid loves this! Grasping the scythe again, he stretches his arms out, twirls round and round, whirling the blade high above the waves of bouncing heads, stomping in his *New Rocks*, marching the dance floor, his pelvis thrust forward, fuckwalking through the crowd. Others join him. Faux-winged fairies rubbing their glistering stardusted bodies against him.

Cupid grins, a superstar grin. Jesus Christ, the boy's got the moves.

Dance, then, wherever you may be;
I am the Lord of the Dance, said he,
And I'll lead you all wherever you may be,
And I'll lead you all in the dance, said he.

76
KISS THE FIRST
The kiss sent the Reaper home to a new source, a zero point, a divine cunt-shaped nothing hole in which to curl. A place where he could do anything, be anything, do or be nothing. A place where he was no longer Death, no longer silent of thought or want. No time space personality. A place of

creation? A place of no thing. This was... what? What was this? Love?

77
CUPID'S KISS

Some of the boys here look like girls. Cupid likes that, it makes him feel strange inside, especially when they touch him. Everyone is kissing everyone else. Boys and girls, boys and boys, girls and girls. A lad with pink wings leaps into Cupid's arms, wraps his slim legs around The Angel of Death's firm torso, curls his arms around his neck. He's wriggling and writhing in time to the music. He's got a mouth like a girl, a wet curl of a mouth. Cupid kisses him, hard. No tongues, it's a vicious kiss. A bruise of a kiss. Cupid likes that. But what he likes best is *her*, that young woman, see her? The one sliding up and down the pole. He throws the fairy boy aside, tosses him into the sea of sweating revellers. Cupid can smell sex. His own. He can smell everyone else's too, but especially *hers* – the girl on the pole.

He slides his hand slowly up the scythe's thick handle, and slides it slowly down again. The scythe is part of him. He's got more wood than is good for a boy. His cock aches.

Guess who Cupid wants to fuck now? Fickle bastard, he is. He's forgotten about Christina. No matter, she's a bit busy.

78
CHRISTINA

Christina was trembling in the Reaper's arms. She felt small, even frail, to him, but everyone would feel small to him. Seven foot of man who'd not yet felt he really was one. Holding her. Holding her up. She might faint. He really thought she might shake herself unconscious and fold to the floor. He's beautiful, the white of his hair like moonshine in the dark of Christina's house. He's beautiful in this pure state of knowing that he isn't what everyone thinks he is or once was.

70

79
CUPID AND THE GIRL

She's looking at him. The girl on the pole is looking directly at Cupid. She has beautiful eyes, green as chemical flame, framed with dark lines of paint, long whip-like lashes. Are they real, those eyes? Do real people have eyes that colour? She has beautiful everything: beautiful dark hair, an athlete's body, tight flat stomach, wonderful biteable buttocks, a very pretty tattoo in script – Angel – and the swollen breasts of a goddess. Are *they* real? Do real people have breasts like that? Cupid suddenly remembers suckling his mother teats, she's got a fantastic pair of jugs, his mum, but then she would have wouldn't she, she's Venus, she *is* a goddess.

80
VENUS

The planet Venus is getting restless. She wants to show her shadow on the sun.

81
CHRISTINA

Christina moans when the Reaper kisses her neck, *he* moans when he kisses her neck, she moans when he moans.

It's a new sound.

He's never heard himself sing this song before.

He wants to kiss her on the mouth, he wants to...

Then she does it.

Shaking still, she puts her tongue in his mouth.

She very gently puts her tongue in his mouth.

To court Love is to stare Death in the face.

82
BRYONY SENDS OUT AN INVITATION

Would you like to come to a party on June 8th? It's Venus day.

Venus is coming

Bryony presses *SEND*.

83
CUPID

The girl's still looking at him. It's lock down. Those eyes. Oh fuck, those eyes. Cupid doesn't care about the spangly fairy boys and silly girls; he flicks them away like flies. He's only interested in the girl who's dancing the pole, she impresses him. How does she do it? She's almost in flight but is wingless. She's upside down, her legs wrapped around the pole, sliding to the floor in this energetic embrace. Shit, he can see the outline of her pouting pussy through the shimmering second skin panties she's wearing.

And as she mounts the pole again, rubbing herself up and down it, legs open, Cupid thinks, I could do that, I want to do that, and he mirrors her movements.

Cupid rides the scythe as the girl rides the pole. It's a merry-go-round-go-up-go-down-and-up-again of lust.

The scythe is part of him. His cock *really* aches now.

84
BREATHE

Breathe.
Can't?
Try.
Yeah, he's hot, isn't he? Cupid.
So's she. Angel.

85
KISS FOREVER, HOWEVER LONG FOREVER IS

Christina could kiss the Reaper forever. However long forever is.

86
STALKER RECEIVES AN INVITATION

Would you like to come to a party on June 8th? It's Venus day.

Stalker already knew it was Venus day. He'd already made plans.

Yes, he'd love to come. Of course, he'd love to.

I'd love to come, he says in an email. And he puts three kisses, too. x x x Stalker presses *SEND*.

87
DANCE

And they dance, Cupid and the girl – synchronised – reflecting each other's moves.

He's every bit as adept on the rod of the scythe as she is on the pole. He doesn't miss a move. It's like she's testing him, her own acrobatics becoming ever more intricate, more convoluted. The flesh of her that is exposed is slicked with oil, golden. Cupid moves the scythe closer, and closer still, holds his hand out to the girl, an offer for her to join him.

She does. She slips from the pole and sashays toward him. Together they ride the scythe, dance its length. It's like they've become one. A single entity, dancing the same dance.

His cock frees itself from the constraints of the belts; his fingers slip her flimsy panties to one side. And he's inside her. It's still a dance they're dancing, but a different dance, one he's no longer lord of, she's commanding him, riding him. Pushing herself down onto his cock, sliding up again until she's almost released him only to lower herself lower, take him deep and ever deeper.

They fuck up and down the well-smoothed wood of the scythe's handle. Some girls in the crowd cry with envy. They'd have loved a bit of Cupid. Some of the boys cry too, for the same reasons. Cupid fucks the girl harder. She cries for more. She'll get more; he's got so much more to give. But not yet. Not with these gawping voyeurs watching. The perverts. Cupid wants to go somewhere private.

88
SIZE MATTERS

It's a shock. Christina laughs and cries when she sees the Reaper naked. This is the Story of Oh!

Women are never satisfied, he thinks. I'll make it bigger next time.

Christina no longer wonders how long forever is. She knows now.

99
CUPID LONGS FOR SILENCE

They're in a private room above the club. Cupid and Angel, the pole dancer. The music is still thumping up through the floor, but it's distant as a memory and everything feels more real now.

There's an unmade bed with a dirty handmirror left on the stained pillow, a sidetable with a drawer and a cubby hole filled with what look like well-thumbed magazines, a lamp with a tasselled shade casts a green sickening glow out into the room.

The girl stares at Cupid, slips out of her panties and the matching bra. She seemed more naked with them on than off. Her tits really are phenomenal, though.

"Take your wings off, babe," she says to Cupid.

Oh. Oh no. Her voice is all wrong. Cupid didn't expect that. She looks like a goddess, speaks like a crone. The voice is thin, impossibly thin, impossible that it could come from a mouth as full and sensual in appearance as hers. She does the bum swaying walk towards him, starts undoing his belts, but his cock's wilting.

"Put the flippin' tool down," she says, her hand on the scythe's handle. That voice is putting out his fire. "You've got a really fit body you have, very sexy." She peels her eyelashes off and flicks them onto the side table. Her eyes no longer look beautiful, but bald and merely salacious. "I exercise to keep in shape, Pilates and that, aerobics, and the pole, obviously. D'you do that sort of thing yourself?"

"No." says Cupid. "No I do not. I just think myself into any shape I want to be."

"Oh right," says the dancer, rolling her eyes. She keeps talking but Cupid's not listening, he's zoned out, she's just making a droning noise.

Cupid wishes she'd shut up.

Cupid won't take his wings off, they're part of him. He won't put the scythe down, that's part of him too.

Cupid says, "I won't take my wings off, they're part of me, I won't put my scythe down, that's part of me too."

"You're a weird one, you are. What the bloody hell are you, like one of them Role Play nutters or something?" asks the girl in the loathed voice.

"Death," says Cupid. I am Death. I am the Angel of Death."

For the first time he really believes he is.

100
THE EXACT MEASUREMENT OF FOREVER

Forever is sixteen inches long. At least sixteen inches feels like forever.

101
WHO'S COMING?

Venus is coming.

Amy and William have cum, are cumming again.

Daryl's lover isn't coming to the Venus day party, Daryl still doesn't know this.

Bryony's going to wish she'd been more careful what she'd wished for one day, and that day is nearly upon her. That day is nearly upon them all.

Christina is cumming. Yes she is. Reaper gives her the biggest little death she's ever known.

CUPID'S SCYTHE
(GRIM'S BOW)

BOOK III

CUPID'S SCYTHE

(GRIM'S BOW)

BOOK III

JUDGEMENT DAY & REVELATIONS

CHILD OF GODS

The girl's eyes aren't green any more. She went to the bathroom and when she came back they were brown. The witch.

"You gonna fuck me properly or what, then?" The voice Cupid has quickly grown to despise is talking at him again.

"Please don't speak, *please*," says Cupid. The boy's eyes are suddenly as tired as a man's.

"Like that is it? I see," says the voice, grating. The naked girl opens the small drawer in the side table. She pulls out a ball gag. "Want me in this?" she asks. "Will that do it for you?" She opens her lips, puts the garish red ball in her mouth, holds the straps behind her head. She poses there for a while, chest thrust forward, legs apart. Her wide eyes expect an answer. Her nipples now look aggressive and misplaced. Are they drawn on?

Cupid shakes his head and looks at the floor. There are cigarette burns in the carpet, the smell of sweat and piss and cum, neither his nor hers. "No," he says. Just no.

The girl throws the gag on the bed. Now she's removing her hair extensions, great hanks of shiny black. She throws these on the bed too. She's looking at Cupid's cock; the voice is coming out of her mouth. "I'm only trying to help; you've gone a bit... off the boil. Been drinking?"

"No, says, Cupid. Please, please, *please* don't speak. I can't stand it. Your voice, it's, it's horrible. I hate it. It wounds me."

No matter what guises we guise ourselves in, no matter what image we choose to adopt, what roles we decide to play, what tools or accessories we opt to toy with, we are essentially what we are, what we have always been and were born to be, we can be nothing else. Cupid is a child born of gods, spawned of the divine potent seed of Mars in the supernatural nurturing womb of Venus, birthed from the sanctified non-human core of her, is it any wonder his sensibilities are scarred by things that are less than beautiful?

Cupid thinks himself a change of image. His white hair grows, a fall of ice, until it is waist length and hangs like a veil against the black of his folded wings. His eyes flash every colour of the spectrum, settling on electric dragonfly blue. He must have beauty, he hungers for beauty.

The girl had pleased him when she danced; the illusion was there, only to be shattered by the harsh scraping sound of her voice.

Just because someone is aesthetically displeasing, it's no reason to try to kill them. You know that, we *all* know that. Cupid didn't.

It's a quarter to five in the morning. The sun is rising. It's a new day. 8th June 2004.

SPEAK ILL OF THE DEAD

"I was terrified of your father," says William. He's holding Amy close to him in her bed.

Bill's snoring, curled up at their feet.

"You weren't the only one, I certainly was," says Amy. "I think even God was."

"Is he, are they, I mean, your parents... are they still... "

"They died. They're both dead," says Amy, as if she can't quite believe it. She kisses him.

William kisses her in return, kisses her again, and again.
"Best not speak ill of them then," he says.

"I don't see why we shouldn't, they can't hear us."

It's a quarter to five in the morning. The sun is rising. It's a new day.

8th June 2004.

REAPER AND CHRISTINA

Christina can't stop laughing. "Oh you are funny," she says to the Reaper. "You can't really have thought it was too small! Not seriously."

"I wasn't sure," says the Reaper.

"Oh stop it, you great twerp!" says Christina, slapping the Reaper's buttocks. "You're just fishing for compliments."

The Reaper laughs now, and holds Christina in his arms.

It's a quarter to five in the morning. The sun is rising. It's a new day. 8th June 2004.

VENUS IS COMING

It's a quarter to five in the morning. The sun is rising. It's a new day. 8th June 2004. Venus is coming.

DARYL

It's a quarter to five in the morning. The sun is rising. It's a new day. 8th June 2004. Too early, Daryl supposes, for her lover to have sent an email or a text, or to have called.

BRYONY

It's a quarter to five in the morning. The sun is rising. It's a new day. 8th June 2004.

Bryony's received an email.

He'll pick her up in the morning. From her place.

STALKER

It's a quarter to five in the morning. The sun is rising. It's a new day. 8th June 2004. Stalker's just going over some notes. Preparing things.

81

HOW TO NOT SAFELY LOOK AT VENUS
Recipe For Disaster – Part 1

You will need:

2 sets of surgical ophthalmic speculums
2 sets of eye droppers
Jewellers' forceps/tweezers
1 pair of sunglasses (optional)
1 woman

Ingredients

- Tropicamide
- Phenylephrine
- Anaesthetising drops

Method

Ensure the eyelids are retracted with the use of ophthalmic surgical speculums or jewellers' forceps (tweezers). Administer a generous dose of *Tropicamide* and *Phenylephrine* combined. The former (*Tropicamide*) will block the pupillary constrictor muscle. The latter (Phenylephrine) will stimulate the pupillary dilator muscle. For good measure apply a liberal splash of anaesthetising drops to the now forced open eyes. This will prevent the eyes recoiling and rolling up in the sockets when they are required to look directly at the sun.

DEATH AND THE MAIDEN

The sun is slowly rising. It's a new day. 8th June 2004.

"You've changed," says the reviled voice. "Your eyes, your hair." The girl is shaking.

"So have you," growls Cupid. "*Your* eyes, *your* hair."

The girl tuts. "D'you still want to fuck or what?" She looks at his cock again, raises her eyebrows, "Or is it a tired boy, is it sleepy?"

The clubbers are still clubbing below. The day can't creep into this fake environment. It's night forever down there. The girl jiggles a bit to the beat of the music, heard still as a distant irritating thump. Cupid wishes she wouldn't move. It makes her tits look wall-eyed.

Cupid flicks his cock with his finger, then slaps it from left to right, sinister-dexter, with a violent swipe of his hand. "Sleepy?" he says. "No, it's not sleepy. It's dead. You killed it. It's death. *I* am Death." He laughs.

There's a turnabout, that's something the girl has never seen before, a guy laughing at his own dick.

Cupid reaches past the girl and grabs the smeared handmirror from the pillow. Holding it against his cock he says, "See, it's died, no breath, nothing. He throws the mirror against the wall, it shatters and the girl flinches. He pulls on his flaccid member, whacks it with the back of his hand as if it isn't a part of him. It isn't. But there's something that is. The scythe. His scythe. Cupid's scythe.

Crying is not a safeword.

WILLIAM AND AMY

The sun is still rising, slowly. It's a new day. 8th June 2004.

"Marry me." William and Amy say the words in unison.

"Yes," they say together.

There's no time to waste. Or is there? Maybe there's going to be all the time in the world. They just don't know it yet.

Amy now believes in love, silly unreal love. Amy now believes love should be forever, just like Christina. "We're here for a blink of an eye, Will," she says, "and when my eyes finally close, yours is the face I want last to have seen."

REAPER AND CHRISTINA

Cupid's in trouble. Reaper can feel it. Something's changed in him, he feels protective, paternal. He feels... love. Love, that old devil. Things have all turned about, things have changed, something's not right. Reaper feels the dread like a disaster warning in his soul. Ha! Does he even have a soul?

No matter what guises we guise ourselves in, no matter what image we choose to adopt, what roles we decide to play, what tools or accessories we opt to toy with, we are essentially what we are, what we have always been and were born to be, we can be nothing else. The Reaper is death personified, he was once and still is the obdurate king of that bleak eternity, is it any wonder his sensibilities are scarred by the thought of Cupid in pain, in danger. Well, actually it is a wonder. Surely the Reaper isn't supposed to be so sensitive, so attuned to man or fellow myth god's feelings. But he's changing. Maybe he isn't essentially what he once was.

"I have to go," says the Reaper to Christina. Only fake flowers last forever. "He's in trouble. I can feel it."

"Who's in trouble?" says Christina.

"The boy, the… *Cupid*. My lad. My little lad."

Reaper no longer cries dry tears.

The sun is still rising, slowly. It's a new day. Day of days. End of days. 8th June 2004.

DARYL

The sun is still rising, slowly. It's a new day. End of days. 8th June 2004. It's too early to lay the table with fruit.

BRYONY

The sun is still rising, slowly. It's a new day 8th June 2004.

Bryony will wear a white dress today.

STALKER

The sun is still rising, slowly. It's a new day 8th June 2004.

Good. There's an email from Bryony. She's agreed to wear a white dress. The Stalker likes that.

CUPID'S SCYTHE

"You want a piece of me?" screams Cupid. His hands are gripped firmly on the rod of the scythe. It's between his legs; the blade rises up behind him, from between his buttocks, a gunmetal iron shark fin.

The blade has every act of annihilation tooled into it. He swung the tool to achieve this phallic stance so violently he cut a spray of dark feathers from his wings, sliced through fine bones, filigree veins and intricate musculature.

Blood of black and bone of white
Feathers dark take unflown flight.

Cupid spits in his palm, acts out wanking the scythe's handle. "THIS, is part of me," he says, snarling and vigorously jerking the tool. "This is a piece of me. Still want some?"

At last he's managed to render her mute. The girl says nothing. He's killed her cock-killing voice. Only her eyes speak; the pure language of tears.

As he kicks her to the bed Cupid cries too.

Cupid cries for shame.

And some shall cry for fear. And some shall cry and beg for more. And some shall cry for the beauty of this beast shall make them cry. And some shall cry with envy.

And one will cry for him to stop.

STOP.

Crying is not a safeword.

The sun is still rising, slowly. It's a new day 8th June 2004.

Day of weeping.

WILLIAM AND AMY

Silent. Forehead to forehead. In love. The sun is still rising slowly. It's a new day 8th June 2004.

CHRISTINA

Do you think the Reaper will forget about Christina now? Wrong. He won't forget. He'll never forget. He'll remember forever. How long is forever?

Christina gives the fake flowers more fresh water. She looks at the dainty bow and arrow the Reaper left on the bed. Such pretty things, sweet of him to leave a little something behind. Mementoes of their time together. Perhaps he'll come back for them.

The sun is still rising, slow as slow as slow. It's a new day. 8th June 2004. Day of days. Dawn of forever.

THE REAPER

Reaper doesn't feel right. He feels like neither Death nor Love. Something is wrong.

He's forgotten the dainty bow and arrow. He feels powerless. Without the tools of his or any god's trade he is weakened, made momentarily mortal. He cannot fly or transport himself in any way other than a man's way, by walking down streets, getting to where he wants to be by taking the long step by step time constrained path of humankind. Slowly, plod by plod. It feels like forever. How long *is* forever?

Take an arrow from an archer; he's no longer an archer. Take god status from a god, he's just a man. Reaper wanted to feel like a real man. Now he does. At least that's what he thinks.

DARYL

The sun is still rising, slowly. It's a new day. End of days. 8th June 2004. It's still too early to lay the table with fruit.

BRYONY

The sun is still rising, slowly. It's a new day. End of days. 8th June 2004. It's still too early to call Daryl and ask if it's all right if she brings a friend.

STALKER
Recipe for Disaster – Part 2

Bake blind.

THE TRANSIT OF VENUS

The sun is still rising, slowly. It's a new day. End of days. 8th June 2004.

The transit of Venus will commence at approximately 05.20 GMT with the black disc of the planet's shadow appearing against the bright backdrop of the sun, our star.

The phenomenon will continue for about six hours.

CUPID AND THE MAIDEN

"I am the Angel of Death," says Cupid. He parts the girl's legs with the tip of the scythe's handle. She jumps and he prods at the wet pink flesh of her, manipulates her lips open with deft movements, achieving unbelievably delicate actions considering the weight and size of the tool. He sees her clitoris shudder.

"You like that?" he says, spitefully. He doesn't expect her to like it, or to answer, doesn't want her to, and she obliges him by not doing either. She is silent. A marionette of raw meat, a thing of flesh.

It's his artful gentleness, his measured consideration, his innate skill, that make his actions so sinister. Pushing the handle an inch deep inside her he says, "How much of me do you want? How much can you take? Does size matter?"

Two inches.

And withdraw and in again.

Three inches.

And out again – all the way out.

And then four.

She moans.

Five, six, seven.

It's a good number, 7. Shaped like a scythe.

Eight.

Nine.

Ten.

Eleven.

Twelve.

A foot of unyielding wood.

Thirteen– Unlucky for some.

Fourteen.

Fifteen.

Sixteen.

How long is forever? How long before she bleeds? Or dies?

Eighteen.

Twenty.

Twenty-four.

Her juices have marked the handle, darkened it. It's a dipstick that shows her oil levels, it's a marker, a tool for measurement.

Cupid fucks, on and on, in, out, in, out. The girl is unflinching, her eyes are open and unseeing, she's spread on the bed, there's blood on the bedspread.

"I can do this for hours, I never tire, I am a god. I'm no sleepy boy," screams Cupid through tears. "I'm a filthy little fucker, nothing can stop me." The words come in gasps, in time with the thrusts. He's losing rhythm now. "I am the Angel of Death and I'll fuck you so hard you'll no longer want to live," says Cupid, his voice cracking, brittle. This is the utterly heartbreaking sound of a boy's heart breaking.

"Help! STOP!" he cries, he weeps, he bawls.

But crying is not a safeword. There is no safeword when you are your own tormentor. Or is there?

"Someone stop me," begs Cupid.

The girl can't hear him.

And then… as if by some magic even he cannot understand someone does stop Cupid. Someone stops Cupid with one sweep of his hand.

It's an expansive hand; a hand with the span of a predatory bird's wing, an elegant long-fingered hand that can block the light from a moon, or dim a sun. It's a hand that can wring equally effectively a strong or a fragile neck.

The sun is still rising, slowly. It's a new day.

End of days.

8ᵗʰ June 2004.

Venus is coming.

WILLIAM AND AMY

Time seems to have slowed. William and Amy, romantic pair that they are, want to watch the sun rise. But the sun seems not to be progressing in its ascension, it's rising, at least they think it is, but will it ever be risen? Has time stopped?

Things are changed, things are all turned about.

The sun *is* still rising, but very slowly. It's a new day. End of days.

8th June 2004.

CUPID, DEATH AND THE MAIDEN

The Reaper lifts Cupid by the scruff of his neck off of the scythe, away from the girl. Some of the new grown fall of ice white hair comes away in the Reaper's hand. He lays the trembling boy on the filthy carpet. He's reclaimed his tool. Cupid's scythe. The Reaper's scythe. It feels larger than he remembered. He'd forgotten its weight, its might, its supremacy. He's almost afraid of it, but there's grim work to be done here, so he takes it once more as his own. The scythe is part of him again.

The girl has died; it's too late for her. She let fear claim her before fight could save her. The Reaper pulls the blood-soaked bedspread around her, to afford her some dignity. He closes her eyes, they look beautiful, he thinks, a rich amber brown. He wipes a sweaty strand of hair from her brow. Poor little thing. Angel.

Cupid twitches and convulses like a shot-down beast. His eyes are no longer as tired as a man's, but they are red with pain and as frightened as a child's. Without the tools of his or any god's trade Cupid is weakened, made mortal and it hurts. The Reaper kneels beside him.

"Oh, you stupid boy," he says, his voice unsteady. "Damn you, you stupid, stupid boy."

The Reaper checks Cupid's wings. They are badly damaged, torn, sliced, bloodied, a dislocated mess of sticky black blood, damped spiked feathers, bone shards, weeping twisted veins. So complex in their formation that wrecked they can only be irreparable. Flightless bird.

"*Stop me*, please," the broken voice of the heartbroken boy pleads in a whisper. "I want it all to stop."

"Yes," says the Reaper, "I know. I know you do."

He enfolds the wounded creature to his chest. He watches the wickedness wash in tides in its eyes until there is none, just a purity as clear as a heartfelt wish.

"Am I broken?" asks Cupid.

"Yes," says the Reaper, "you little fool." He feels the creature's panicked heartbeat fluttering in the cage of its ribs. He removes its leather wristbands, its skull rings. They are not part of him.

𝔉or we brought nothing into the world, and we can take nothing out of it.

The Reaper unbuckles, unzips, unchains and pulls the ridiculous hefty boots from the boy's feet, massages his swollen heels, the bruised blackened toes, the red raw sore ankles. How the crazy kid had managed to fly in these boots, hell only knew.

"Ah." The Reaper sighs. "Determined little devil you were, strong too," he says, looking deep into the fallen angel's eyes, kissing his forehead, stroking his hair, holding both his shaking hands in one of his own. "That's my boy," he says, "my beautiful precious boy."

And in that moment the Reaper understands what it really is to have to be a man rather than to simply want to be one, and weeping the un-driest tears a man has ever shed he wrings the fragile neck of the boy Cupid.

The sun has stopped rising for a moment. It's a day on hold. End of days. 8th June 2004. Venus will cast her shadow on the sun. Venus will appear soon, as shady and dark in grief as a widow in weeds.

CHRISTINA

Christina puts the dainty bow and arrow next to the vase with the fake flowers in it. She doesn't realise the sun has stopped rising. She doesn't know it's a day on hold, a morning in mourning. 8th June 2004.

DARYL

Daryl feels like the world is coming to an end. She's not far wrong. Love is dead. Love was nothing more than a boy with wings. Love is now an unbreathing child in the arms of the Reaper. The sun has stopped rising for a moment.

8th June 2004.

BRYONY AND THE STALKER

Bryony can't wait to meet the Stalker. The Stalker can't wait to meet Bryony.

The sun seems to have stopped rising. The Stalker has been watching the rise with interest. It's odd. Something's not right. That's because things have changed, things have all turned about.

CUPID – REAPER – DANCER – BOUNCER

The Reaper lifts the limp flightless bird body of Cupid, the corpse of Love, up in his strong arms, and drapes him over his right shoulder. He will wear the dead boy as a king wears robes. Blood drips slowly from the soft arc of the boy's open Botticelli mouth, the head lolls from the snapped and twisted neck. His eyes now stare blind at the filthy floor in the filthed room.

"I'll take you away from this," says the Reaper, straightening his back, broadening his shoulders. He bangs the fuck end of the scythe on the floor, asserting himself, assuring himself of his reclamation of his tool, his role.

"Here we go, Cupid, hold tight," he says, to the boy who can't hear him. He is glad Cupid never had to see him cry. He wouldn't have wanted to be a disappointment. The Grim Weeper.

The clubbers never seem to stop. The music is still thumping itself numb below. The day never seems fully to shoot its load. The sun is still fucking refusing to rise. It's raining, pouring with rain. Venus is crying a million tears. Her primal scream, the howl of a mother's loss is felt and heard as thunder. The shock of her intense grief is represented by the unexpected spear of lightning that fractures the sky.

About to descend the stair the Reaper meets the bouncer heading up. He's looking for the girl. The pole has been undanced for too long. Where the hell is the stupid bitch?

It's Cupid the doorman sees first. "Out of it, is he?" he says to the Reaper. He rolls his eyes. "These kids wanna learn to water their juice down." Then he sees the scythe. "Devious little shit. I told him he couldn't bring that thing in here. He your lad is he?"

"Yes," says the Reaper, proudly without hesitation, "he's my boy." Weeping still, he descends the stair.

The doorman's in the room.

"What the fuck? He's shaking the girl loose from her bloodied shroud, shouting her name. "Angie? *Angie?*"

"Oi! You! You fucking bastard. Wait!" He calls out to the Reaper, stumbles down the stair's first few treads, eyes red with rage. "Wait! I fucking know him, I know that kid. He's the killer. He's the one. He killed the seven. I saw him. He's killed Angie!"

Finally he's recognised Cupid. And he leaps, all six thickset feet of him, down the stairs.

"I'll fucking *kill* him," he yells as he jumps onto the Reaper's back. The man's a savage; he bites the Reaper's neck, he roars.

But he can't kill Cupid. Cupid is already dead.

And he can't bite or roar or shout anymore. He's falling in half – cleaved through by the scythe.

The Reaper wears the corpse of Cupid like a kingly robe and the raw burden of the halves of the doorman as he walks through the sea of bouncing writhing sweating dancing bodies in the club.

And some shall cry for fear.

The hysterical mass moves as one, people don't know what they're doing or why they're doing it, some are jumping up as the Reaper passes, they clutch at Cupid's feathers. They all want a piece of him. Girls are crying and hiding their faces. The bouncer's carcass is leaking blood over the dance floor.

The boy with pink wings whom Cupid had kissed is wide eyed with fear and amphetamines. He's out of his mind. He waves a gaudy plastic crown in the air, and calls out to the Reaper above the still relentless thump of the music. "Dude," he shouts, "He won this! Best costume. He's the King of the Angels, the winner of the best dressed Death competition. Everyone reckoned his was the bollocks. Sick, man. Hands down."

And the Reaper stops, stands still, in the midst of all the chaos, a terrible Jesus parting the red sea of bodies that is red with blood. He stops and raises his hand and the music dies. And with imperial grace he takes the garish crown from the boy with the pink wings. "Thank you," he says, "he would have loved this."

Well, well, thinks the Reaper, a feeling of inordinate pride warming his bones. The boy done good. He won something. Then, dropping the dead meats of the bouncer's body on the dance floor he says simply, "It's been lovely. Farewell."

Reaper is only seen if he wants to be seen.

He can hear sirens.

Time to move on.

The Reaper hates goodbyes.

The sun has stopped rising for a moment. It's a day on hold. End of days. 8th June 2004.

Venus is coming. Venus will cast her shadow on the sun. Venus will appear in widow's weeds.

THINGS HAVE CHANGED
THINGS HAVE ALL TURNED ABOUT

On a remote plot of land, empty but for a faded sign that reads "Planning Permission Applied For" the Reaper settles the body of Cupid in a patch of buttercups and cowslip. He surveys the area. It's as good a place as any. He doesn't care that some day houses might be built here.

With the scythe that is now very much a part of him again, the Reaper effortlessly digs a grave. Churning the wet earth, disturbing the worms and insects that will soon be a part of him too, and a part of Cupid.

The star that is the Sun is watching. The planet that is Venus can't bear to. Not yet.

The Reaper places the gaudy crown on Cupid's head. It sits unevenly on the boy's thick tumble of white hair, juxtaposed against the Klimtean Kiss angled head on the broken neck. The glass jewels, the candy coloured representations of emeralds and rubies catch in the still sultry light of the morning.

The Reaper, with Cupid's kingly head nestled in the crook of his neck, his arm about the boy's waist and his other hand in determined possession of the scythe, steps into the grave and lays down. It's deeper than other graves and longer and wider.

The Reaper feels the wet warmth of the earth against his back, smells the deep smells of its rich fertility. He looks up at the sky, the sun is rising. He closes Cupid's eyes with a kiss to each and then with the scythe he triggers an avalanche of dirt which floods into the pit covering him and his little charge, the late little king of kill, newly crowned, the recently deceased little love god. It will be peaceful for him, thinks the Reaper. At last.

The Reaper himself will know no such peace. He cannot die.

And the planet Venus cries again.

And the rain of her weeping washes the remaining mounds of the Earth's earth into the grave where Love lies silent in everlasting slumber in the arms of the Death that cannot ever die.

Things have really changed now; things have really all turned about. The sun has risen. 8th June 2004. It's a new day.

VENUS IS COMING

Bryony phones Daryl to ask if it's all right to bring a friend to the Venus day party. It is. Amy phones Daryl to say there's been an ever so slight change of circumstances; it's not just going to be her and the dog. "It'll be the three of us now," she says. She's never been able to say that before. It's always just been just the one of her. Amy.

Daryl is arranging fruit, Arcimboldoesque style as planned, and aphrodisiac foods, (asparagus and chocolate) on the garden table. The weather's been unpredictable this morning but it's now settled and it looks like it's going to be bright this afternoon after all. Her heart's not in this, it's not in it at all. No news from her lover. She's contemplating cancelling the party, but she doesn't want to let her friends down. So she'll pretend she isn't breaking, she'll smile and pretend not to be going slowly painfully insane. Even in this tender state she wants to champion love, as if love is a cause to be championed, a worthy pauper in need of a "Friends of" clan whose benefactors would rattle cans and beg donations and signatures for petitions.

Even when love is nearly killing her, she cannot kill love. You'd have to be really harsh to do something as soulless as annihilate love on Venus day, wouldn't you? Too late. Love is already dead.

Christina misses the Reaper. She'll miss him forever.

WHAT HAS CHANGED EXACTLY?
WHAT HAS ALL TURNED ABOUT?

Everything has changed.
Everything has all turned about.
EVERY. SINGLE. THING.

4, 2, 1, AND -1

Four women, two men. One dog. One woman missing - Daryl's lover, she's not coming, she's definitely not coming.

$$4 + 2 + 1 + -1 = 7.$$

It's a good number 7, shaped like a scythe.

The Stalker has introduced himself as Jude. Bryony's fallen heel-over-stupidly-romantic-head in love with him, at first sight. That's one wish granted. He's gorgeous, Jude. Just her type. She always did prefer blond gentlemen. Everyone thinks Jude is very handsome, even Daryl, who gave up men a long time ago.

Christina wishes she'd brought the dainty bow and arrow with her to this party; it would have made an appropriate prop for such a day. She never asked the Reaper why he had so peculiar a thing with him, at the time it just seemed right that he did. Why question everything anyway?

Amy and Will are getting on the others' nerves, kissing all the time, focussing only on each other and occasionally on the dog Bill, who is pulling at the table cloth and growling a growl that's bigger than he is at Jude.

So here they all are, the friends, together again. Only they're not really together, no one really notices what any one else is doing, no one feels what any one else is feeling. There are the polite sounds of wine glasses chinking and small talk being talked and small tinkling surges of lame laughter whenever anyone tells a joke that isn't particularly funny. These are the noises humans make to kill the enemy that is silence. These are the sounds they make to soothe.

No one notices that Daryl cries at everything, and if they do notice that her lover hasn't turned up they don't mention it – too uncomfortable. No one notices that the fruit, so beautiful, so ripe, so sweet scented, is served on a writhing bed of maggots. No one notices that the chocolate is melting. They don't eat the asparagus. Just as well, it makes your piss stink. No one notices when Jude takes Bryony by the hand

and leads her to the summer house at the end of Daryl's garden. No one notices that he carries a rucksack on his back, or wonders what he keeps in it.

Venus is coming. Soon.

PERPETUAL BLOOM

So where's the good in all this?

Where are the happy endings?

Are there any?

Is there ever going to be an end to anything?

Well, Amy and Will, they're in love, that's a keeper. All the Reaper's doing. He was proud of that.

Bryony? It looks like she got her wish, doesn't it? Does it? *Really*? He's a Stalker, the man's a psychopath. We know this. You've known it all along. Only Bryony doesn't, yet. Fuck's sake, even the little dog gets that there's something not right, something obscure about Jude. Don't fall for his golden good looks, his charm. How shallow. So who did this to Bryony? The Reaper, Cupid? It was a little bit of both of them. Too many cooks.

Christina. The forever thing? Another wish granted. Well done the Reaper. She's like a fake flower herself now. In bloom, in perpetual bloom.

Daryl. She always knew love could send you crazy, nothing's changed. Descending.

What else?

Anything?

Oh yes, there's the little matters of Death having resigned and Love being dead. So apart from three of Cupid and the Reaper's guinea-pig-crash-test-dummies, Amy, Bryony and Daryl, everyone else in the world is now immortal, including Christina, she's got her forever now. Everyone else in the world is now unable to love.

That's everyone.

EVERY. ONE - EVERY. SINGLE. ONE.

Everything has changed.

Everything has all turned about.

THE UNIVERSE IS WRITING
ITS LAST WILL AND TESTAMENT

The Universe is writing its Last Will and Testament. Strange time to think of it, just as this megaton 'Every Thing and Every One is Forever But No One Can Ever Love' spell has been cast. But the Universe is ancient, old school, the Universe is a traditionalist. Better the devil you know. The Universe bequeaths the planet that is the Earth to the meek. But things have changed, everything's different now and the meek reject this inheritance.

We do not want this throne,
Of a debauched killer king in a jokeshop crown.
This earth of pale unmajesty,
This unwiped piss-dribbled toilet seat of Mars.
This smothered auto-asphyxiated ball-gagged Eden.
This dull unpleasing paradise.
This fortress built by wicked Supernature,
For the supernatural,
To promote foul infection,
Amongst what once was a happily unhappy breed,
Of women and of men.
This little world.

We do not want your fragile unhatched speckled egg of Earth,
Your failing rock which, when viewed from above,
Shows crawling maggots, Humankind,
Deprived of Death and Love.

The meek can be quite overblown and poetic when roused. Who'd have thought it?

They could have just said, "We don't want this world in which no one ever dies and no one ever loves. It sounds like it's going to be a pile of shit."

To live forever…

…to love never…

is death.

RUCKSACK

Checklist of things in Jude's rucksack:

- 2 sets of surgical ophthalmic speculums
- 2 sets of eye droppers
- Jewellers' forceps/tweezers
- 1 pair of sunglasses
- Tropicamide
- Phenylephrine
- Anaesthetising drops
- A photograph of his mother.
- Rope
- Duct tape

SUMMER HOUSE

The walls are the colour of winter in the summer house.

Jude the Stalker is pleased to find there's a chair - very useful.

VENUS IS COMING

At long last. Bloody hell, the hype surrounding this shady business has been really over the top, long winded. This'd better be good. C'mon Venus, get your tits out for the lads.

JUST HOW IMMORTAL IS EVERYONE?

People will be expected to live and age up to the point at which they would have naturally have lived and aged, until their number would have been up, only it never will be, like in a nightmarish surreal version of Bingo where you never get to shout Full House. Then they will simply stop ageing and never die. Suicide will be impossible although some people will attempt it just because it'll be something to do - bit of a laugh. Invincibility will turn some people into total cocks. Still, the ever more elaborate jumpings from tall buildings and hangings and failed drownings will become Internet fodder for the bored masses and become so popular that people will forget that there were once cats that did the sorts of things cats do, or babies who, amazingly, laughed or whatever it was that once captured the world's tame imaginations.

Only Amy and Will, Bryony and Jude, and Daryl are destined to live out the expected number of human days. Oh, and Bill, the dog, and the cat Vienna. But wait, there *is* someone else who'll die one day; just as they all will eventually, in time. Almost forgot about her. She doesn't know it yet, but she's pregnant.

No conceptions take place after the day Death resigned and Love died. But babies conceived before 8th June 2004 will be born. Sex thereafter will be a non fruitful non-loving dissatisfying act, which kind of explains why the suicidal art of non suicide will take off. People must have their petty thrills.

VENUS IS HERE

As if you need reminding:..

The transit of the planet Venus is an extraordinary and arresting phenomenon you simply won't want to miss - however you must observe safety guidelines. Don't let the mandatory warnings alarm you! You can experience the transit of Venus in safety, but it is imperative that you protect your eyes at all times with the use of proper solar filters. NEVER stare continuously at the sun. Take regular breaks and give your eyes a rest! And remember, sunglasses don't offer sufficient protection to the eyes.

So, if someone, if some twisted fuck were to follow parts one and two of a self fashioned recipe for disaster, what would happen?

It doesn't bear thinking about, no need to go over the list of ingredients or the gory details of the method again, the proof as they say, is in the pudding.

Six hours later. There's Jude, The Stalker, with Bryony, the woman with her hair on fire and her white dress stained with vomit, coming back up the garden path. Her pupils are blown, her eyes burned. The result of six hours of the sun's intense infrared rays scorching down on them. *Six hours.* Way over the top. Fifteen minutes of flame would have done the trick. Bryony's staggering, can't see where she's going. It's all right, Jude's there to guide her, the blond leading the blind, up the garden path. An uncarefully wished wish. Love at first sight. And at last sight too. She'll never see another's face again. A wish granted is not necessarily a dream come true.

VENUS HAS GONE

Bye bye, Venus. Bye for now.

14TH FEBRUARY 2005

It's a girl. Weighing in at:

- 3175.1469939 grams (g)
- That's 3.1751469939 kilograms (kg)

or

3175146.9938999997 milligrams (mg)

or

- 111.99822997463225 ounces (oz) which is, as you probably know, equivalent to 101.6047038048 Troy ounces (ozt)
- In Pennyweights (dwt) 2141.6195170777
- She'd be 15875.7349696 Carats (ct) were she gold
- 194.31899602668 Ticals
- 84.649441885737399 Mommes
- 48992.51811587702 Grains
- 28.5763229451 Newtons

In Singapore, China and Hong Kong Taels she's:

- 83.82388063896
- 84.45891003774

and

- 82,5538218414

Or for those of you listening in the good old fashioned British past:

- Seven Pounds. 7lbs.

It's a good number 7, shaped as it is, like a scythe.

The baby is beautiful; they pick her up from the hospital when she is just seven days old. They tell Donna she's welcome to stay in touch if she wishes. Donna doesn't wish to. There's money to be made with TV interviews and magazine features. Sad tales of how she had to have her baby adopted seeing as the father, one of the Seven Angels, was dead. William and Amy call the little baby Rose. She's a lucky little baby, this one, to serendipitously land in the care of the only two people left in the world who are truly in love and are truly able to love her. And love her they will. She will grow to be a beautiful child.

Sometimes that happens, something pure from evil comes, something exquisite is grown from a filthed origin. It gives you hope, doesn't it?

DARYL

Daryl can still smell madness, she can smell it now, this fresh madness all her own. It is her own un-solid state she is detecting. Love, after all, *did* send her crazy, this she knows. She is irrevocably in madness now. LOVE, it can be etched, scrawled in blueish black, across the knuckles of a thug. It can be present, like a watermark, through your soul. It can be many things, mostly indescribable. Truth is it's only possible to write of love in the blood of gods with the quills of angels. Even then, words don't always live up to expectation. And anyway, where can such blood and feathers be found?

Blood of black and bone of white
Feathers dark take unflown flight.

102

They will be here to inject her soon. And they'll wake her to give her her sleeping pills. Until then, she sleeps safely, curved like a pupae in her madwoman's bed, her dulled head lolling chestward, her arms wrapped like straight-jacket straps around her torso.

CHRISTINA
Christina never buys fake flowers anymore. Real ones last forever, as will she. She still misses the Reaper.

BRYONY
Bryony wishes every day that she'd been more careful what she'd wished for.

2670 DAYS AFTER THE DAY ROSE WAS BORN
It's the 6th of June 2012. Rose is 2670 days old today.
That's:
- 230,688,000 seconds

or
- 3,844,800 minutes

or
- 64,080 hours

or
- 381 weeks (rounded down)

or
- 7 years, 3 months, 24 days

When asked Rose always rounds down and says she is seven. All together now...

"It's a good number, 7, shaped, as it is, like a scythe."

Rose is good with numbers. She's not so hot on spelling which worries Amy, but doesn't concern William. Amy thinks Rose has learning difficulties. Amy's wrong. Watch...

They're at Christina's house. She invited them round for a little get together. They weren't really sure what to do on such an anniversary, an anniversary of death and so much sadness, such carnage. Spending it together seems the right thing to do. The only thing to do.

Amy says, "Will thinks I worry too much, about Rose. But you just do, as a mother."

"It's dyslexia that's all," says William. Many of the world's greatest writers have suffered with dyslexia. Hans Christian Andersen, Agatha Christie. F. Scott Fitzgerald. Gustave Flaubert. Yeats.

Amy laughs. "It's her own name she struggles with the most. She keeps spelling it S, E, R, O, Sero, bless her. And she's such a tomboy."

Rose says, "Can I play with this please, Auntie Chris?" The child has found the dainty bow and arrow.

Christina nods. "If it's all right with Mummy and Daddy."

It is all right with Mummy and Daddy. "In the garden though, darling, and be careful," says Amy, "it might be sharp."

William says, "Let her be, let her have some fun."

In the garden the child laughs. "Silly Mummy, silly Daddy," she says. "I *can* spell; I can spell all my names."

And in the dirt, in a dry summer-scorched patch of earth the child uses the point of the dainty arrow to make her marks.

S, E, R, O, Sero.

And then… R, O, S, E, Rose.

Then very slowly she inscribes the letters in a turned about way:

E, R, O, S

Eros.

Laughing again, she sets the arrow against the bow and aims it at the sky, at the sun, at the sun the planet Venus plans to show her shadow on. She draws back the bow and fires…

… and…

… the arrow sails the skies, flies the crow's way toward its destination. The arrow knows exactly where it's going.

When the arrow lands it frightens the mythical horse, Paradise and he rears up on his hinds legs, like a lion rampant on the humble unmarked grave he has stood vigil over these seemingly endless years.

When the arrow lands, in the earth that tops the humble grave in which Death and Love are entwined, a bush grows, as if conjured up by a deft magician's hand. It is a bush in bud. A rose bush.

And a breeze carries an everlasting stormstream of red petals up up up above the grave, to the skies. This bloodbird flock is seen from below as a shapeshifting swarm.

The petals spread, converge and hang heavy in place of the sun for a while and then form a simple hopeful symbol; a heart shape that rose tints the world.

It is 6th June 2012. Today the planet Venus will show her shadow on the star that is the sun and things will change. Things will all turn about.

**"From my rotting body, flowers shall grow
and I am in them and that is eternity."**

Edvard Munch

ACKNOWLEDGMENTS

Mister William Farrow: for being a true friend to me and a supporter of this book. He is solely responsible for the inclusion of the obligatory whelks in Book I of *Cupid's Scythe (Grim's Bow)*

Professor Dan Z Reinstein, MD MA(Cantab) FRCSC DABO FRCOphth FEBO: for his invaluable input regarding my ophthalmic research which was largely 'Googling stuff about eyes' before he came to my rescue.

Mister Richard Blacktarn: for his expert opinion and constructive criticism and encouragement.

Mister Cameron Holroyd for his insightful and sometimes startling suggestions about *Cupid's Scythe (Grim's Bow)*.

Mister Roger Povey for reminding me that Hope was fond at the bottom of Pandora's Box. This has served me well in both real life and the sometimes even more real realm of fiction.

Mister Milton J Shapiro – remembered.

Venus De Mileage

Printed in Great Britain
by Amazon.co.uk, Ltd.,
Marston Gate.